D0329721

BAD BOSS CHICKS 2

PERK THIRTY

Cole Hart
SIGNATURE NOVELS

Bad Boss Chicks 2

Copyright © 2020 by Perk Thirty

All rights reserved.

Published in the United States of America.

All rights reserved. No part of this publication may be reproduced, distributed, or transmitted in any form or by any means, including photocopying, recording, or other electronic or mechanical methods, without the prior written permission of the publisher, except in the case of brief quotations embodied in critical reviews and certain other noncommercial uses permitted by copyright law. For permission requests, please contact: www.colehartsignature.com

This is a work of fiction. Names, characters, places, and incidents either are the products of the author's imagination or are used fictitiously. Any resemblance of actual persons, living or dead, businesses, companies, events, or locales is entirely coincidental. The publisher does not have any control and does not assume any responsibility for author or third-party websites or their content.

The unauthorized reproduction or distribution of this copyrighted work is a crime punishable by law. No part of the book may be scanned, uploaded to or downloaded from file sharing sites, or distributed in any other way via the Internet or any other means, electronic, or print, without the publisher's permission. Criminal copyright infringement, including infringement without monetary gain, is investigated by the FBI and is punishable by up to five years in federal prison and a fine of $250,000 (www.fbi.gov/ipr/).

This book is licensed for your personal enjoyment only. Thank you for respecting the author's work.

Published by Cole Hart Signature, LLC.

Mailing List

To stay up to date on new releases, plus get information on contests, sneak peeks, and more,

Go To The Website Below...

www.colehartsignature.com

TEXTING LIST

To stay up to date on new releases, plus get exclusive information on contests, sneak peeks, and more...

Text ColeHartSig to (855)231-5230

1

Mob $hit

SUMMER HAD PLENTY OF "SEXCAPADES" in her life, but she'd never had sex on an airplane. But like the saying goes, there's a first time for everything. And there she was, on a Gulfstream G550 Jet, flying over the Atlantic Ocean on her way to Italy. And she was *seriously* getting her back dug out.

"Oh, shit! Angelooooooo. Mmm, baby...that...feels...so... damn...gooood," she moaned.

"Say what darling? Tell...me...how...this...big cock feels in your tight black pussy," Angelo said. He dug his fingers into Summer's fleshy backside and pounded her out doggystyle. She was bent over the butter-soft leather seat, reclined at a 45-degree angle. Angelo crouched over her back with his feet on the floor, and he rhythmically sawed into her dripping wet pussy with long, heartfelt strokes. Summer bit the headrest and enjoyed the sensation of getting her fallopian tubes poked.

Angelo was hung like a horse; the real definition of an "Italian Stallion."

He loved the sight of the waves he made in her ass whenever he slapped her booty cheeks. After getting shot, Summer had lost her perfect bubble butt, so she had it surgically repaired and altered. Now her ass was bigger and better. The best money could buy!

"You love this Italian sausage, don't you il Mio Amore?"

"Oooooh yes. I *love* it."

"Whose pussy is this? Huh, whose is it?" he demanded.

"Ahhhhh shit. Angelo, this is your pussy Daddy. Oh, fuck! Yesssssss," she moaned.

Angelo stuck his thumb inside of her crimped bootyhole, and she came instantly! Her pussy spasmed and released a flood of juice, coating his dick with thick white cream. Her puckered asshole clutched around his thumb, squeezing and contracting his finger tightly while she orgasmed. "Huuuuunnnh, ahhhhh," she screamed at the top of her lungs as she looked out the window at the cotton candy clouds floating by. *What a way to join the mile-high club*, she thought to herself as Jeremih's song "*Planez*" featuring J. Cole popped into her head.

A few minutes later, Angelo busted a hellafied nut deep inside of her pussy. They both collapsed on the peanut butter colored seats, gasping for breath, and sweating like they just ran thirty miles!

"Summer, you are one hell of a woman my dear," Angelo said, stroking her damp skin.

"Mmmm, thank you. And you baby, are *ALL* man," she cooed. She bent down and took his semi-hard, slimy dick into her mouth. Summer sucked on her pussy juice and licked his left-over cum off. His toes cracked as she made them curl. He palmed her head, lifted his butt off the seat, and clenched his ass cheeks tightly together.

"Grrrrrr," he growled, his eyes rolled to the back of his

head. Angelo had never seen a woman so passionate, freaky, and beautiful in all his life. Then again, he hadn't messed with many American women either. And the ones he did, were nothing compared to Summer Thompson. He knew from the moment he laid eyes on her in Zurich, that she was a keeper.

After Summer and them did the mass murder at the rappers' mansion, she decided to disappear from the states for a while and do some world traveling with Angelo. Everyone on the East coast was on edge, and it was really hot in New York because of what went down. Plus, with Becky getting knocked, all of the Tekashi69 snitching shit, and other WTF situations going on, shit was crazy to her. And even though Summer wasn't a suspect, she felt it would pay off to be seen in other parts of the world and not in hip-hop hangouts, in case the streets were talking and putting two and two together.

Summer adored Angelo. When he found out she was shot, he flew to the states to be by her side in the hospital. He kept asking her and BBC how he could help, while also demanding to know who tried to assassinate Summer. She wouldn't tell him because they were gonna take care of it on their own (which they did). But still, it was sweet of him to be so concerned. She saw him in a whole new light during that ordeal. Besides her girls, he was the only one holding her down. He also paid for that reconstruction surgery to fix the flaws the gunshots did to her body.

During her stint in the hospital, she got a chance to truly reflect on her life. She'd never been incarcerated before, but laying up in that hospital bed made her feel like a prisoner. She couldn't go anywhere or do anything for herself. And like a prisoner, when one has nothing but time on his or her hands, she couldn't help but think about things.

Even with all of their money and success, they were not immune to hardships and real-life drama. And bullets could have *anyone's* name on them. Summer knew she was no saint.

She'd done a lot of dirt. Set up muthafuckas, robbed, stole, murdered, committed every sin under the sun. She repented when she talked to God daily, but she knew she was done dancing with that bitch "Karma" when she came knocking at Summer's door.

It was something a lot of people in the streets ignored or failed to accept. When you're out there doing dirt, you're gonna get paid back for what you do someday. In one way, shape, or form, Karma will come back to slap you in the face and tell you, "*That's for that bullshit you did*," so don't bitch or cry when shit happens to you. Wanna play the game? Be prepared for the consequences that come along with it. Just as you prepare for and fully accept all the rewards and shine that comes along with it too. It's a two-way street. And no matter who you are, every dog has its day. But to Summer, a strong, independent black woman from the streets, she had the Mil in her blood. Milwaukee muthafuckas didn't give two fucks! And that's how she felt. "*A minor setback for a major comeback* " is the philosophy she adopted during her recovery. When she got out, it was a new and improved version of herself. She had a new lease on life and a different agenda than that of the *old* Summer.

Angelo had his own jet, and their first destination was to his native homeland. Summer had been to Naples, Rome, and Milan (for fashion week of course), but never to Sicily. He was born in Palermo, where the *real* syndicate originated. She was excited to meet his people and soak up their Italian culture.

He took her to his mother's house, a tastefully decorated mansion where an elaborate home-cooked dinner was laid out for them. Summer really hit it off with his 31-year-old sister Helena. She was a funny, green-eyed beauty with olive skin and jet-black hair that hung to her waist.

Angelo's mom Gloria was a sweet, compassionate woman who spoke little English. She was a "family first, loyalty or nothing" OG of a woman. Summer won them over right away by just being herself.

Angelo had two younger brothers who were twins. They got killed a few years prior, "casualties of war" is all he told her, as she looked at family photos and portraits of the Moochinis in their living-room.

After an exquisite Italian dinner of beautiful stuffed Porchetta, Tagliatelle Genovese, Butter sage Gnudi, Hunter's Chicken Stew, and tomato courgetti and basil pizza, they drank glasses of Nino Bellini-Veneto, talked openly, and laughed a lot. Then Summer and Helena had fun trying to teach Gloria some dance moves and how to "drip sauce."

Summer and Helena exchanged numbers and promised to kick it soon. Angelo and Summer left in his aqua blue Maserati Levante S and headed to his "Bachelor's Palace," as he called it. A 10 bedroom, 12 bathroom mansion, overlooking the Tyrrhenian Sea. M-16 toting guards and leash-less Rottweilers walked the premises freely. Summer was a bad ass Boss Bitch herself, but she knew Mob $hit when she saw it.

Every room had marble floors. Some had marble walls and ceilings. Classic art adorned the walls; Picassos, Van Gogh's, Monet, Warhol, and Basquiat (which impressed Summer because she was a big fan of Jean-Michel Basquiat).

Angelo wasn't a weed smoker, but he was a wine connoisseur, owning hundreds of the most expensive bottles in the world in his custom-made wine cellar. So, while Summer puffed on a blunt, he sipped from a goblet full of Chateau Cheval Blanc 1947.

"The states are so dangerous now. Mass shootings, police brutality against your people, crazy lunatics going nuts and all kinds of crazy shit. Even you, getting shot for whatever reason. A beautiful woman such as yourself should *never* get marked up," Angelo said, stroking the scar on her arm where she took a slug. "I know you're more than just an entertainer and urban model, and that's fine. Really, I admire your independence and ambition. You're tough too. You have that inner *'don't fuck with me'* beast in you that will surface if crossed. I can *see* that in you. I'd never try to change that, or you in any way, shape, or form, but I want you safe sweetheart."

"Angelo, I'm as safe as I can be now. I carry my gun everywhere – "

"I'm not talking about a gun," he said, interrupting her. "You got attacked in broad daylight. Your friends were gunned down like animals!" Summer got teary-eyed. She had their blood on her hands because of *her* actions, *her* schemes. Like Angelo's young twin brothers, her peeps were "casualties of war." She was lucky to be alive. *Blessed* is more of how she felt though.

"And by who? Some fake gangster wannabe's? Jealous, envious haters? You had no security detail, no nothing! No matter where I am, no matter where I go, I have armed guards around, because you never know what will happen in this crazy world these days."

"So, you want me to travel everywhere with bodyguards now? Is that it? Cuz daddy I'm not Whitney Houston."

"Who?"

"Oh my God boy, for real?" Summer smacked her lips. "Never mind. Look – "

"Summer, I've got the best security in the world. The head of my Securities company is ex-C.I.A. I have trained professionals working for me from the Marines and Navy Seals."

"Daddy I appreciate the offer, but I'm not having some big burly ass dudes following me around like some damn puppy dogs everywhere I go," she said, then she hit the blunt really hard, blowing rings of smoke at the beautiful portrait on the marble ceiling. "Is that a Julie –"

"Bell? Yup. *Unfolding Rainbow*. I love her. She's one of – "

"My favorites!" Summer said, cutting *him* off this time. They smiled at each other.

"See, that's why I like you. You have an open mind, and you think outside of the box. You're not a petty, miscellaneous thinker –"

"Nah boo, I ain't no miscellaneous ass bitch."

"I know you're not. So why would you think security is just all dudes?"

Summer's ears perked up at that comment. *He got bitches on deck too?* she thought to herself. "Angelo, what are you talking about? Spit it out daddy."

"You better not spit it out though," he said jokingly. Summer laughed and playfully hit his arm.

"Boy hush, witcho nasty self," she said, then flickered her tongue at him suggestively.

"We'll get into everything later, but for now, come with me. I've got something to show you," Angelo said. They got off the grey suede couch and walked up the spiral marble staircase with the solid gold banister. On the second floor, they got on an elevator, which was the only way to get to the exclusive third floor that contained four separate rooms. He led Summer to the second door on the right. Angelo punched a code into a keypad before getting his retinas scanned by a futuristic looking device on the wall. A series of beeps went off and the vault-like door opened.

There was a small foyer that led to an all-glass room. He opened the door and they set foot into a room that resembled a custom-made gun store. The floor was entirely cheetah skin carpeting. Gold racks and shelves lined all the walls. Assault rifles and military weapons filled those racks and shelves. It was like a Combat room. Summer stood in awe as Angelo slowly walked around the room naming off guns she'd never seen nor heard of before.

Ultramax 100-U, AAP52, M1895, Caltech PF9, Beretta Modello 30, M3P, LAW Rocket Launchers, ZK383, L86. There were also hand grenades, machetes, swords, laser beams, silencers of various sizes, and shelves of ammo filled bandoliers. But what he really wanted to show her was the secret room behind the bookcase of antique handguns. He hit a hidden switch and the bookcase moved to the left, revealing another full-sized room.

It looked like a small department store, similar to Kohl's, but this had the drip of a Macy's. Racks of men's and women's clothing in assorted styles and sizes filled the room. There were suits, dresses, cardigans, jeans, stilettos, boots, sneakers, hats, purses, suitcases, oxfords, ties etc. Summer looked puzzled until he explained.

"Every article in this room is bulletproof. These are specially made clothes and accessories lined in high-quality Kevlar. Have you ever heard of Miguel Caballero?" Angelo asked.

"Um, no. Doesn't ring a bell," Summer replied, shaking her head.

"Well, he's the creator of the keenest, bulletproof clothing in the world. He custom makes Kevlar clothing and accessories for all the big fashion houses: Armani, Versace, Prada, you name it. Look at this, it's an anti-ballistic Polo shirt," he said, pulling a cream-colored Ralph Lauren shirt off the rack. "It costs four grand and can stop an Uzi or a butcher's knife!"

Summer caressed the smooth fabric. It felt like a regular satin/cotton blend polo shirt.

"And this is Kevlar?" she asked in surprise.

"Yep. The best of its kind. The material is made in Milan, the fashion capital of the world as you know. The special Kevlar however is manufactured in Bogota Columbia, the most violent country in South America. Miguel combines the two, and produces beautifully tailored garments that protect... um, those of us who live rather dangerously," Angelo said.

"Oh, so you live dangerously, huh? And here I thought you

were just an import/exporter," Summer said with a smile. Angelo chuckled.

"You are too smart for that Summer. I'm sure you know I'm a made man," he said, caressing her back as he whispered in her ear. Tupac's song "*Made Niggaz*" popped in her head. Her pussy began to tingle feeling Angelo so close to her.

"Mmmm. Made huh?"

"Mmhm. And I'm taking you to Milan so Miguel can fit you for all the top fashion brands. That way, you can move around safely and feel more secure if another incident occurs. God forbid, but I want you as safe as possible. I also will have all of you and your friends' vehicles bulletproofed, with secret compartments installed to stash your weapons and umm, other things, if need be. With your permission, that is."

"Hmm, I don't see why not. After all, it is for my protection, right?" Summer said, dropping to her knees.

"Why, of course darling," Angelo responded as she unbuckled his Gucci belt.

"So, this is bulletproof too?" Summer asked, referring to the belt, before unzipping his pants and digging inside of his boxer briefs.

"Mmhm. But uh, *that's* not," he said, when she pulled his penis out and began licking it like an ice cream cone. "Goodness gracious! You are incredible," he groaned. Angelo ran his fingers through her hair and looked up at the mirrored ceiling. He watched her top him from a top view. Summer felt his praise and compliments warranted an extra treat, so she "Alvin, Simon, Theodore'd" him until he erupted in her mouth. And like the boss freak she is, Summer swallowed every... last... drop!

2

J.O.E

"*Mama prayin' for a safe night, can't die from venom I'm too used to snake bites. All these niggas see is my brake lights. Used to the dark, I never come with a safe light, it goes wrong? It goes wrong; I know that my faith right –*"

"Eeeee, who is *that?*" Becky said, sitting up in her tiny bed in the cold jail cell.

"Oh, girl that's that '*Yes, Lord!*' by Styles P."

"Styles P?" Becky asked, feeling the *can't die from venom/I'm too used to snake bites* line.

"Yeah, dude from the Lox. Stomp down New York nigga."

"Oh, I *loooove* New York. My friend Dee runs shopsnx up in Yonkers," Becky said.

"You know Darrell?" Mz. Queenz asked, surprised at who the white girl knew.

"Sweetie, who *don't* know who's selling the hottest urban books and mags to peeps in the joint? Shoot, my homegirl been in plenty of them mags dudes be jacking off to," Becky said. The women in the cell giggled.

"That's what's up though." Mz. Queenz, a black and Puerto-Rican woman from New York, nodded. They were in a federal holding detention center in northeastern Wisconsin. Women from all over the country were detained there. "You don't look it ma, but I can tell you a thorough ass bitch. A *bad* ass bitch."

"Thanks, Mz. Queens. So can a bad bitch here those bars again?" Becky smiled.

"Oh, that um...mama praying for a safe night, can't die from venom I'm too used to snake bites. All these niggas see is my brake lights..."

"That shit is dooooope Mz. Queenz," Becky said.

"Slinkowsi! You got a visit. Let's go," A crabby female C.O. came to the cell and said. Becky jumped down from the top bunk and slid into her orange jail Crocs. She'd been waiting for this day. She looked in the cruddy mirror and ran her fingers through her hair. On her way out, the women in the cell gave her words of encouragement. They knew how tough it would be.

"I DON'T KNOW who these people you are hanging around with Rebecca but..."

"Dad, you know me. I'm not into none of that shit that bitch stashed in my car."

"But why would she do that Becky?" Gail Slinkowski asked her firstborn.

"Why? Why? Because she's a two-faced, jealous ass, back-stabbing, rat cunt that's fucking why mom!" Becky yelled.

"Shhh, calm down honey. Don't – "

"Don't what, shout? Fuck that shit mom! I get set up, and

my whole fucking life is ruined. All because of some spiteful, snitch bitch." Becky sobbed. Big, angry tears flowed down her cheeks, as the hurt and pain spilled from the eyes that knew too much.

"Rebecca, your life is not ruined. Do you remember when you got into trouble before? We took care of that situation," Tom Slinkowski told his daughter, hoping to comfort her.

"Dad, that was weed. This is a whole other ball game. Look, I'm not even caring about the drugs anyway. You don't understand. This...this incident changes everything..."

"Of course it does. You're all over the front page of the Post-Crescent – "

"I don't care about the papers or the news mom. Jeez, I have a lot more to worry about than your precious reputation. My life is on a timer now. It wasn't supposed to end like this. It wasn't supposed to end like *thiiiiiis,*" Becky dropped her head and cried heavily. Becky could only be vulnerable with her family because they never judged her. She didn't have to put up a front with them. It was the first time that she cried since the whole ordeal, and she let it *all* out. Her family looked through the glass partition and could feel her pangs in their own hearts. It was too much to bear. Becky gathered herself together and said goodbye to her mom and dad so she could talk to Britney. Their parents left the visiting room sobbing in each other's arms.

"Why don't you wanna come home?" Britney asked her big sister. Becky removed the receiver from her ear and pointed it at Britney. Becky shook her head.

"You think I *wanna* be here?" Becky snarled, getting back on the visitation phone. "Because of that *Fuck* bitch Ma Baby, I got a target on my back. I have to sit in here a while so you can study and prepare. And that'll be three to four weeks minimum."

"Study? Three to four weeks? Becks, what are you talking about?" Britney asked.

"By the time I come home, you'll need to know everything there is to know in order to take my place."

"Take your place? You're confusing me," Britney said.

"Jealous ones envy. That's what J.O.E stands for. Some chicks in here taught me that. Do you know the obstacles and hurdles we've had to deal with over the past few months? People trying to set us up and set us back. Foes trying to get rid of us. Motherfuckers doing us dirty. It's all a part of life. Jealous... Ones... Envy. Remember that. It's why you were hashtag trunking motherfuckers. It's why I got rid of some motherfuckers too. Because their envious jealousy did not want to see us prosper. But we weren't having none of that. We acted on their deception and they paid the price, with their life!" Becky's bright blue eyes flashed like lightning.

"It's not gonna stop. The fuck shit continues. Ohhhh does it continue. You don't even have to be in the game to get fucked over in life. Innocent bystanders die all the time from drunk drivers, stray bullets, fatal diseases, and other bullshit. People get cheated on, stolen from, used, lied to, beaten, treated like shit, and hurt every day. None of us are immune to the bullshit is what I'm saying. It can happen to anyone, at any time. But it's up to *us* to be ready for the fuck shit though," Becky said, looking around the visiting room carefully.

"Yeah, I could be home right now, but that would be dumb on my part. The Feds are now about to be on my ass like stink on shit. We have to uproot our whole operation and get the fuck outta Appleton."

"Ok, but where do we go, and what's the next move Becks?"

"Eau Claire. You've never been there, but we own a Salon up there, so I have ties there."

"Eau Claire? Where the hell is that at?" Britney asked.

"An hour and a half from Minneapolis. It's a few thousand

people less than Appleton but pretty much the same culture. I have peeps I want you to plug with up there. We're gonna do the same thing with the schooling shit too. Find some young, passionate girls and take them under your wing. We're gonna fund their education and give them careers."

"Ok, that's no problem, I can do that," Britney replied.

"You have to promise me something though Brit-Brit."

"What's that sis?"

"When you're out there hustling, stay in your lane. Weed is your game. Stick to that. You're gonna network with people who sell coke, H, meth, everything. And the money is great. But the cons outweigh the pros. Too many rats these days. It's hard for people to get a good run in. It'll be appealing, but don't venture off course. Set your goals and chase them. Once you accomplish one, set another. You should never stop striving. Never stop dreaming."

"Becky, you're talking like I'm never gonna see you again. You're scaring me."

Becky smiled. "Don't be scared hun. I'm just preparing you for what lies ahead. Shit is about to change for all of us. We never think the unthinkable can happen to us, until it does. That's your first lesson Brit. You know how Big Brother says expect the unexpected? Well, be able to handle the unthinkable when the time comes. You're young, but you're starting to see just how much life is built on fuck shit. Fuck boys and fuck girls rule the world! Motherfuckers doing the most bogus stuff are the ones running shit. The president, the government, the police, the catholic church..." Becky paused. There were scandals in every denomination, but since they were brought up Catholic (which is the most controversial), she used that as an example.

"Us real motherfuckers are dying or getting locked away, while the fuck people coast through life prospering from there bogusness. Snitches are walking around telling on everybody, and people are still friends with these rats. People are fucking their best friend's spouses and significant others behind their backs. Sex offenders get a slap on the wrist because the judges and D.A.'s are also those same kinds of sick perverts behind closed doors. Once loyal people are crossing their day ones over petty shit. Hell, I know people whose own families, I'm talking about the same *bloodline*, fucked them over," Becky said, shaking her head.

"Life is a bitch Britney. You've only seen a few situations. Deemontay, Amber, the twins, your haters... now this. But there will be more fuckery to come. Trust me; it's coming. It goes hand in hand with the game. If you're out there getting money? Someone is going to try and bring you down. Why? Because they envy you. They want what you have. They feel as if you don't deserve what you've hustled hard for. There is nothing stopping them from getting money and living a good Boss life, except for their lack of passion and Go Getterness. All the time a hater spends trolling, making comments, and spewing hate towards those doing good, could be spent running up a check and securing the bag ya know?"

"Yeah, I feel you. So why don't they then?" Britney asked, not understanding why everybody couldn't eat.

"I told you. Jealous ones envy. We don't all have good hearts. Many are just cold-blooded to the core. Maybe they've been lied to, cheated on, robbed, stolen from, raped, incarcerated, or abused just *too* many times. People grow jaded after going through fuck shit for so long, and eventually it rubs off on them. When you cross the threshold of not giving two fucks about anything in life anymore? You're at the point of no return then. It's inevitable that the person scorned will either do some fuck shit or turn into a fuck person completely. Ya see, we've all done some fuck shit. Fuck shit is something dishonorable. But just because you *do* fuck shit, don't make you a fuckboy. Or a fuck girl. It's what's in your heart that separates you from those kinds of people. If you're constantly bogus, always on some sneaky ass conniving shit, then yeah, you're a fuck person. If you truly want to help others get in a better position in life, show them a good time, and have their best interest in hand, you're not a fuck person. Because you have compassion and empathy. Fuck people don't care who they hurt or offend. Old people, children, the vulnerable, they are all fair game to fuck boys and fuck girls. They have no hearts. They don't give two fucks about anybody! Hell, how can you get through to a person who don't even give a fuck about their own life? If they don't care whether *they* die or not, you think they gonna give a damn about *your* life? Nope. That's why you gotta watch out and be on alert. Those motherfuckers are everywhere Brit-Brit. I'm telling you, it's crazy out there. You're young and have your whole life ahead of you. I just want to give you this game now. Who knows when my time will come?"

"Becky, you'll be home in no time. I don't know why you won't let mom and dad bail you out now. Everyone knows they own businesses. They can afford the $250,000 bond."

"I know. But don't you understand I will be under a microscope now? They're gonna follow me and fuck with me wherever I go. I can't move and groove freely like how I used to. That bitch Ma Baby put a target on my back because of this bullshit. I've been here a minute now, and I'm sure everyone is paranoid wondering what I done told these cocksuckers."

"Yeah right! Becky, everyone who knows you knows you're not a snitch. You're the most loyal, stand-up girl I know."

Becky got teary eyed. Her sister was right. Never in a million years would she roll over on her click. White or not, she was a thoroughbred bitch who kept her mouth closed. Sure, the Feds came down on her like a ton of bricks when she first got knocked, but all she told them was, "I want my lawyer." They never got so much as another word out of her. Now, as she sat across from her sister, dropping jewels and hoping the teenager took heed of the game she was giving her, she was determined to plant the seeds that would not only make her younger sibling a Boss Queen someday but would keep her *alive*. Becky knew she was on borrowed time. Her life was a ticking time bomb, and she was trying to get as much done as she could. She wasn't scared though. Sad, yes, because she hadn't hit 30 yet and wanted to do and see a lot more in life. But one doesn't always get what they want. Sometimes we only accomplish half of our dreams. If she didn't die in a shootout with Ma Baby (because she was at that bitches' head when she got out), she thought the BBC would have her merked. She knew too much, and she thought they would be leery having her around after she spent so much time in Federal custody. And that thought hurt the most because she was 100% loyal to those women. But she knew the position they'd see it from, and she completely understood. Even though she was part of the "fam," Becky was new to the click. They'd kill her in a heartbeat and find another down ass white bitch to take her place. If anything, she'd hope it would be her sister.

"When you get to Eau Claire I want you to link up with Ham Samich."

"Ham Sandwich?" Britney asked.

"No. Ham *Samich*. He's really finicky about people mispronouncing his name. Anyway, he's the leader of the F.N.B'z."

"Wait, does that stand for?..."

"Fuck N Boyz," Becky said.

"They actually named their click Fuck Nigga Boyz? Do they know what a fuck nigga is?" Britney said, scratching her head.

"Oh yeah. That's the shit I'm talking about. It's cool to be a fuck boy now. Motherfuckers are proud and representing the fuckery culture. It's frickin' insane. They got dudes in the F.N.B'z who are documented snitches. Their paperwork is all over the internet, they openly say, 'yeah, I told. So what?' Pure sheisty individuals. They fuck each other's baby mamas and girlfriends behind each other's backs. They run off on the plug – "

"Yeah, but that's dope as fuck tho," Britney laughed, cutting Becky off.

"Are you retarded? Why the fuck would you run off on the buffet that's been feeding you? Um, you ever hear of biting the hand that feeds you?" Becky asked her little sister.

"Yeah, *that's* not cool tho. But you know, 'I'm a run off its ten or mo, run off even if you my bro..." Britney paused as the wheels in her head spun. She had heard so many songs referencing "running off on the plug," that it seemed cool. When in all actuality, it was a "fuck act" to run off on the socket that kept on the lights.

"Look, it's another form of robbery, which is cool if that's what you gotta do. Ya down on your luck and need to hit a lick? I get it. But most of these dumb motherfuckers run off with crumbs when they could've been eating whole pies. If they run off on the plug, they *should* have a better one lined up, because they sure can't go back to the one they fucked over can they? These clowns don't think long-term though. It's all temporary fixes and instant gratification. That is what separates *us* from the rest. We do Bo$$ shit! If it furthers our goals and cements our legacy with generations to come, we're getting it done. But we never, ***ever***, cross each other. It may not be any honor amongst thieves, but you never cross your fam. Evaluate who your truest are. You most likely won't see who those true motherfuckers are until you go through some tough times though. Hey, it is what it is." Becky shrugged.

"At the end of the day, instill loyalty. Create ***REAL*** people you will ride for; the same ones who will die for you. This is not just talk. You see where I am right? Death or incarceration are the consequences if you don't play the game well. Very few get to the top, so enjoy each level you climb as if it *is* your top.

Laugh, flirt, dance, kiss, fuck, take pics with your friends, turn up, enjoy your life to the fullest, and thank God for every good time and every good day you have. Because they will never outweigh the bad ones you suffer through.

Show people a good time. And even if they don't fuck with you after you've blessed them and showed them genuine love, chalk it up as them 'running off on the plug.' It's acceptable to do so these days right?" Becky shook her head.

"Plant the seeds now, because the real are dying off. If they aren't locked up or dead, it's far and few in between of real ass, one hundred, motherfuckers out there. With your fuck culture thinking it's cool to rip off their friends every chance they get, purposely give bitches STD's, impregnate hoes and never see the baby, and all kinds of foul shit; the fuckboy/fuckgirl is no longer just a movement, it's become a *culture*. Like the dudes in Eau Claire you're gonna be around. They fuck N's and represent it proudly."

Britney shook her head in disgust. "I don't know why you won't say the N-word Becks. You're not racist."

"I know. It's just not something I'm comfortable with. I know you say it – "

"Yeah, it's no biggie. It's how you use it. But damn, you like, *really* want me to fuck with a fuck nigga Becky?"

"No, no. Not fuck with like *that.* Just get cool with him. Despite their sheisty ways, these motherfuckers are stomp down killers. They'll pop that thang quick fast and in a hurry. It's always good to keep shooters on your team and keep them close by. So, even though I don't agree with what they stand for, I do respect the fact that they openly embrace and claim to be a -"

"Fuck nigga?" Britney questioned.

"Yes. This way we can proceed with caution and choose how we want to fuck with them. Just know, at anytime, they might cross you. Because, well, they're – "

"Fuck niggas. And that's what fuck niggas do."

"Exactly!" Becky said. "They've never crossed me. They know I'm not a punk ass white bitch. They also know I have deep connections, so they respect me."

"They don't want no smoke!"

Becky laughed at her little sister. "Speaking of which, they hold this Awards show called 'Who Want Smoke Awards' every year up there. It's crazy as fuck. You won't believe some of the categories and shit that goes on in that motherfucker. It's put together by this chick named Lady H *allegedly*. But no one really knows who she is. Anyways, I want you up there in time for that. But remember, there are certified snitches all around, so make sure you let a cocksucker know you ain't no punk ho." Becky stopped and looked at her sister who began to shed tears.

"I miss you, Becky. I want you home. This isn't fair!"

"That's another life lesson Brit-Brit. Who said life was supposed to be fair? Kids get Cancer, homeless families go hungry, and that shit sure isn't fair, but that's reality. Lots of things happen that shouldn't happen. Fuck it, what can we do but play the cards we're dealt and try to get motherfuckers like Bill on our team to help us when shit like this happens," Becky said. Bill Shultz was an Appleton cop and close friend of the family. He always gave Becky the heads up if she or her family came up on the radar in his jurisdiction.

"We fucking hate the oinkers, but he's one right? And he's fucking mom, so she obviously likes him too," Becky said. They both laughed, knowing all too well that their swinger mom was banging a local sheriff.

"Networking is key. Knowing people in different places, that are good at different things, is always beneficial to a hustler. Remember that. But never get close enough unless you are prepared to use your stinger."

"Stinger?" Britney asked.

"Yeah. Did you know that when a honeybee stings someone, it can't pull its barbed stinger back out? Attached to that stinger is the abdominal, digestive tract, muscles and nerves. This big abdominal rupture kills the honeybee."

"Ummmmm?"

"Beez will sting your ass knowing they're about to die. I'm a Bad Bee now. It's the path I have chosen for myself. So, whatever comes along with it, I need to accept it whole-heartedly. It's ride or die for me Brit-Brit."

"I'll ride or die for you Becks."

"I know you will hun. But I don't want you to worry about any of that extreme stuff right now. You'll be eighteen soon. Enjoy being a teenager. Time flies by because life is short. One day you'll look up and be like, where did all those years go? For people in here, it can be paralyzing. Brit-Brit, you have your whole life ahead of you, so soak up the game and knowledge I'm giving to you. It will come in handy at some point."

"Oh, I'm soaking it all up. I know I have a lot more to learn but – "

"This is a good start. Another jewel is it's not who you are, but who you *know*. That's why networking is so important. We need people in high places just like we need people who aren't looked at as valuable, but they *could* be. That fat kid at McDonald's might make a good runner, *and* he'll give you free fries. So, don't treat him like a pee-on, put him on. Show him how to eat. The same way I showed you. The same way mom and dad showed us. The way my Beez have taken my minor league thinking to the majors. You'll get there someday. It's in you. You're destined for greatness."

"Wow, you really think so Becky?" Britney asked, blushing from her sister's words.

"I sure do. And I'm gonna make sure you're an even *Badder* Bitch than me!"

"Heyyyyy now," Britney said, getting all excited.

"I wrote the girls and explained everything already. You'll

be glued to GG's hip for the next few weeks, so once they say you're ready, I'll bail out and we will go from there."

"Ok Becks, I trust you. Even though I don't like the idea of you rotting away in here –"

"Rotting? Awww, come on. I get three hots and a cot a day, don't have to pay no bills – "

"I'm being serious Becky, jeez."

"I know, I know. Just trying to make light of the situation. It sucks, but hey, I'm meeting some big-time plugs in this motherfucker, so it ain't all bad. I'm around bitches who are really doing it, that's the kind of company I want to keep."

"It's doing you no good in here though," Britney said.

"True. But it's only for a little while. It'll give me just enough time to get in good with the connected chicks in here so we can have more outlets for our team. Until then, I'll be reading, working out, meditating and praying for better days ahead."

"There are all kinds of 'Pray for Rebecca' groups and petitions online."

"Wait. Really?"

"Yeah. Like hundreds of our church friends shared posts to their friends. Different people in the Outagamie community who've come to the salon for years have been rocking **#Free Becky** shirts, hats and other shit all over the city. Everyone sees it as a conspiracy against a successful, *affluential* family."

"Affluential?" Becky laughed. "Well, at least they don't think we're some drug dealing murders. So that's good."

"I know right?" Britney laughed.

"For reals. When you get home, I want you to send some love to a few people. Send them some flicks and tell them to keep their heads up. Chico, TK, Twan, Des, Kanari and Munchie. They're some good motherfuckers in a fucked-up situation."

"Ok. Anything else?" Britney asked her older sister. It was creepy to stare into the same eyes that she saw in the mirror every day. But it was comforting to know that she had some of Becky inside of her.

"Let GG mold you. Follow everything she tells you. These are lessons you can only learn hands-on. So put your all into everything you do from here on out. You have to take the reigns and hold shit down for now. It's a lot of responsibility, but this is what you signed up for. So either piss or get off the pot."

Britney nodded knowingly. "KK. I love you Becky."

They said their goodbyes and Becky went back to her cell hoping her little sister would take heed to all the advice she gave her. All she could do now was hope for the best.

3

Who Want Smoke?!?

"Yo, this is the wildest shit I've ever seen!" Bucky said excitedly. Britney had been in Eau Claire, Wisconsin for three weeks. They did things a lot differently than Appleton did, and Bucky was right, they were wild as fuck in Eau Claire!

Britney had set-up shop with her S.B.G'z after meeting up with Ham Samich and the Fuck Nigga Boyz. They were cut from a different cloth, but she got along with them just fine. Eau Claire boasted their own version of street muthafuckas. The same street muthafuckas who voted for their peers at the Who Want Smoke Awards. An annual ceremony that celebrated those getting it the best in their chosen fields.

Britney (who just went by the name "Brix" now), invited Bucky and his Pill Mobb click to accompany her to the Awards show. She told them she wanted some muthafuckas from Appleton to rep with her, but she also had other reasons. It was held at the Expo Center on a cool Saturday evening. Bucky was geeked because they just saw two nominees whoop each other on the red carpet with Brass Knuckles.

They were deep in that bitch. Brix, her man Gutter, her right-hand woman Tanya, ten Snow Bunny Gangstaz, The BBC (minus Becky), and a few members each from THOT Gang and TLB were the arm candy for some of Pill Mobb.

"That bitch put the smackdown on that nigga!" GG said, holding Bucky's hand. Two nominees for "Best Hands" decided to duke it out on the Red Carpet. A six-foot-tall mulatto chick named Pearl G ran up on Rhino, a big, black ass, ugly nigga, and told him she was leaving with the trophy one way or another.

"Bitch, please. I done knocked out mo muhfuckas this year than you did," he told her.

"Nigga, what the fuck that mean? You ain't knock out nobody important! I put the floo-flops on Bizzle, Dawn, Gage, and I smacked the shit outta Trell and his bitch ass ain't do shit. What, you beat up Kyle's meth-head ass?" Pearl G laughed in Rhino's face. "And pussy ass Chopper? Hmpf. That shit shouldn't even be *recognized.*"

"Get your hating ass out my face ho. You don't want no smoke," Rhino said and muffed her in the face.

Pearl G, quick to react, punched him in the throat. Rhino staggered back and held his neck where her fist connected. Pearl used this opportunity to pull her 24 karat Gold Brass Knuckles from her purse. Once they were on her hands, she pounced like a Kangaroo.

"Yeah, you a big nigga." **WHAP! WHAP!** She two-pieced him in the eye and mouth. "But nigga, I'm more of a Gangsta than you'll *EVER* be. That's why they call me Pearl *G*. You gonna respect my *Gangsta* nigga!" **WHAP! WHAP!** She fired off more punches to his ear and jaw. Guns were the only weapons not allowed at the Who Want Smoke Awards. Anything else was fair game though, including: brass knuckles, knives, bow and arrows, whatever.

Rhino's homie tossed him a pair of brass knuckles and he stepped to Pearl G like the animal he was named after. The two went blow for blow, but she definitely had the upper hand on him. Attendees looked on in awe. Cameras recorded the footage, and security made sure it was a one on one "fair" fight.

Rhino caught Pearl with a hard right and knocked her to her knees. This was the perfect opportunity for her to strike from the position she was in. Like Ryu on the Street Fighter game, she did a rising uppercut (minus the "Shoryuken" sound effect) straight to his balls. This caused him to double over in pain, *big* mistake. She went Tasmanian Devil on him and tore his ass up! Pearl G left him on his back for his boys to pick up.

The peeps in Eau Claire had their own style and different kind of drip, so the red carpet wasn't as glamorous as Brix would've liked. Summer, Rose and GG were looking hot as always. But she was no slouch either in her sky blue Badgley Mischka off-the-shoulder dress and heels. The weeks spent with GG had paid off. She now knew how to walk in heels *and* carry herself more ladylike. She was still an Air Force One's and Jordan's kind of girl, but GG showed her the swag a woman had to have while dressed in her evening best. Anyone watching Brix from the back would swear it was Becky. Brix had her big sister's walk and mannerisms down to a Tee.

In their short time spent in Eau Claire, they already cemented themselves as a powerful and influential click that a lot of people gravitated to. Besides the F.N.B'z, Brix had gotten cool with Ari, the head of the Blonde Champions, a click of young hustling bitches. Then there was the Lil Onez, six "little people" who had the plug on all things artillery and were quick to pop shit.

Card $quad was a team of professional gamblers who tore off casinos and were the best at winning any game you could play for money. They were very smart, keen individuals who knew their stuff. ZayFocused (the leader of Card $quad), was a cool ass dude from Milwaukee. He taught Brix how to play craps one night.

They were all in attendance. This was the biggest event in Eau Claire's history, so it brought the city out. Pretzel Bitez and her Gang of BBW's were turnt up. Nappyhead, a local rapper and producer, was sipping from an $8,000 bottle of LOUIS XIII Magnum Remy Martin as he hit on every woman he saw.

"...*Now it don't take much to get a bitch gone/Five bands on your head send you home/late nights and we creeping to the moan/Cuban Baby yeah I'm sitting on my thrown.*" The rapper Cuban Doll opened the show with a slew of her hits and got the crowd turnt up.

"Y'all give it up one more time for Cuban Doll. She going hard on muhfuckas." The crowd erupted in applause and whistles, showing the pretty rapper mad love as she exited the stage.

"Hey Rose, can we get her at my birthday party?" Brix leaned over Gutter and asked.

"Si Mami. We'll make that happen for you," Rose replied.

"Thanks, ma. I really like her." Brix said.

"Yeah, me too. She's a beast!" Rose responded.

"Welcome to the third annual Who Want Smoke Awards. The craziest award show in the muthafuckin' world!" Perk Thirty, the host of the show said into the microphone. "Shiiid, we done already had some epic shit go down pre-show on the red carpet. A fuck nigga got his paternity test results served to him. TJ, you are 99.9% the father muhfucka. Now, are you gonna be the ultimate fuckboy and abandon it? Is he or she gonna be a bastard, because *your* dumb ass, chose to nut in that nothing ass bitch? *Yo* bad," Perk Thirty laughed. "Orrrr, are you gonna be a stand-up dude for once in your fuckboy life? Who am I kidding, we all know the answer to that right?" the crowd roared with laughter; they all knew of TJ's reputation and what he would do.

"Shout out to my Body gang niggas. From the Mil to the EC. Orrr... did y'all see this?" Perk Thirty pointed at the giant screens behind him. Jamie, a "Best Head" nominee, was filmed on the red-carpet servicing two big dicks at the same time. "The bitch is cold y'all. Look at her go!" The camera zoomed in on her giving a first-class blowjob to two lucky men. She even winked at the camera while doing so.

"And Rhino, you are automatically disqualified from the Best Hands category. Pearl G knocked you out fam. So, if your name *is* in the envelope, she wins by default." Perk Thirty shrugged. "Your hands ain't better than hers homie.

By the way, if I don't win Best Drip, I'm slapping me a muthafucka! Y'all know ain't nobody fuckin witcho boy in the drip game," he said, and the crowd laughed lightly.

"But for real tho, I'm honored to host the only award show put together by the streets, where the winner is also picked ***by*** the streets. Whoever you are Lady H, good lookin' on funding such a unique celebration of the hustling culture. Just like the trap museum in Atlanta, the Who Want Smoke Awards is in a league of its own when it comes to street recognition. It's gonna be some bragging rights earned tonight! So, without further ado, let's kick this shit off and see who the real winners are. Welcome our first presenters. He's a good Mil-town friend of mine, and she's his ride or die dime. Killa Kane and Sassy Ass."

The crowd clapped as a tall handsome brother and pretty blonde chick walked up to the podium. He wore black Gucci pants and a button-down shirt, with a black Milwaukee Bucks hat tilted to the right. She wore a black Gucci mini-dress and red bottom heels. Her lips were adorned with pearls and diamonds that sparkled brightly. He puffed on a blunt while he spoke.

"Every year, a bunch of hungry individuals take to the

streets with a vengeance," Kane said and blew smoke into the microphone.

"Their goal? To get their motherfucking paper and put their loved ones in better situations," Sassy Ass continued. "What I like about these four nominees, they are *all* women."

"Not just any women tho babygirl. These women are the top Go-Getterz in the city. These are the four chosen ones who have been crowned by the streets as the top hustling Queens. This year's nominees for Best Female Hu$tler are... Kayla B." The crowd clapped as Killa Kane read Kayla's bio. "This multi-colored hairdresser is a sexy, single mother, who works full-time, takes care of a farm, and still finds time to sell everything under the sun that will make her money grow."

Sassy ass read the next nominee. "Ari, the leader of the Blonde Champions. She has been making a lot of noise this year. The youngest of all the nominees, Ari has managed to build a money getting team of beautiful hustlers. She gets her hands on whatever your heart desires and looks good doing it."

"Pretzel Bitez. You know I got a lot of love for you ma," Killa Kane said. "This woman has been an Eau Claire staple for some years now. She even beat out all the big-time niggas last year when she took home the Hustler Of The Year Award."

"Last but not least, Gibbler. You showed the heart of a lion when you took over your man's empire and held him down when he got knocked. As a square, you got hip to getting your money real fast. From the bar to the hospital, to the BioLife Center, you chased your cash and made sure those that you loved ate good," Sassy Ass announced.

"That's real shit yo," Kane said into the mic while Sassy Ass grabbed the envelope. She made sure the crowd saw the *KB* on her French Tip nails that were trimmed in diamonds. Those motherfuckers were on fleek, and she knew it.

"Yeah, ya dig. This that muthafuckin' understand me right

here. The boss chick that really gets her gwop," Killa Kane said. Sassy Ass opened the envelope and looked over at her King.

"Ari!" They both shouted in unison. The pretty blonde looked stunned to hear her name called. She stood and smoothed out her dress. As she headed to the stage, she flipped her long blonde hair over her shoulder. Camera flashes sparkled like stars under the spotlight that followed Ari to the podium. She paused to throw up a BC for her girls.

Looking bad as fuck in a strapless royal blue champion dress, she stepped to the mic in thigh high leather boots with Blonde Champions written all over them.

"Yo, I can't believe this shit," Ari began, accepting the unique looking trophy from Killa Kane and Sassy Ass. "I just got on my grind for real for real this year. After life smacked my young ass around, I decided to get serious about my paper. My bitches Chloe, Kiana, Natalia, Makayla... ganggang!" The Blonde Champions click stood up and shouted "GangGang" while throwing up BC's. "Y'all know what we been through. It's all love, no matter what. Y'all my day ones til my last day. Love to my fam and everybody who showed me love and never tried to fuck me over. Death to anybody who crossed me or don't like me. BC Biiiiiiiiiitch!" Ari shouted before walking off holding the trophy high.

Everyone clapped, even the other nominees who felt they deserved to win. But what competitor *doesn't* want to win? The next award brought GG and Summer to the stage.

"A lot of bitches suck dick. I suck dick. *She* sucks dick," Summer pointed at GG. "Every bitch in this arena sucks dick. And a few of you niggas do too," the crowd laughed.

"But the bitches in this next category, go above and beyond your average blowjob," GG said. "To win the best head award, you have to be –"

"One hell of a cocksucker!" Summer finished saying.

"And the four whores whose mouths have been cum dumpsters and fuck holes for the year are..." GG said, then turned to look at the screens behind her. Each nominee was introduced with footage of her skills. A husky-voiced woman was the voice-over for their bios.

"Missy, the cute Native-American with tattoos from the neck down, who's down to give neck and go down, whenever and wherever. Praised for her great ball licking technique, they say she is among the elite fellatio givers in Eau Claire county.

Tangy Tongue. The heavily pierced BBW whose tongue is said to always have a tangy citrus flavor to it. That's because her specially made tongue ring squirts a heating liquid full of tingly Vitamin C that energizes and makes men's toes curl!

Jamie, the purple hair, coke-bottle figured, aspiring model, has been cemented in dick sucking history after taking on 108 dicks in one night! A record she set in a rowdy frat house on Water Street after Country Jam this year.

And Victoria 'Cumgirl' McGee, the petite beauty whose Suck fast/swallow hard motto has become a popular trend with the up and coming top givers."

"Daaaaaaamn," GG said in shock after watching the nominees in action on the big screen. "All you bitches need to holler at us after the show if y'all get down like *that*. We'll make sho y'all get paid like a muthafucka."

"Hell yeah. Sucking all that dick for free. Hmpf," Summer said and shrugged.

"Some just want the fame tho. And now, the bitch that sucked the best dick," GG began.

"Had the coldest cocksucking skills," Summer continued as she opened the envelope.

"Heyyyy! The winner is the bitch that was getting down on the red carpet. Jamie, come get your well-deserved trophy ma," GG said.

Jamie was 5'6" and thick as a muthafucka! She switched her hourglass hips as she strolled to the stage. Her bright purple hair hung to her fat ass. An ass she made sure everyone saw in her tight mini-skirt. She wore a purple fishnet piece that concealed only the top half of her booty cheeks.

The Who Want Smoke trophy was two hands twisting up W's, and the pinkies were connected. A blunt shaped like an S had wafting smoke that billowed up between the W's. GG and Summer handed the trophy to Jamie.

"I've been sucking cock for many years now. Love sucking and always will. It brings me joy and gives me pleasure to see that look of pure bliss on a man's face because of what my mouth is doing to him. I feel powerful, yet appreciated, even if he don't give a fuck about me, he's loving my spitty ass mouth when he's in it. I get pleasure from giving pleasure, plain and simple. Get chy'all suck game up hoes!" Jamie said, and did the – dick poking the inside of her cheek move– with her hand and tongue.

The crowd applauded as she exited the stage. Last year's winner of the Best Booty category came to the stage next. "For those of you who don't know me, I'm Biscuits," the thick woman said as she turned to the side. One hand on her hip, she showcased a perfectly round butt in her neon green leggings. "I was Best Booty 2019. And even though I'm not nominated this year due to the rules, I still think I have the best ass in the Midwest." Chants, barks, and whistles came from the crowd. "But this ain't about me. This is to see which four women have been voted best Booty by the streets. This year's contenders are..."

"Samantha P. This big booty vixen is the mother of two, runs a CBD shop by the mall, and has an ass every man stops to do a double take at.

Nicole S. Strapped to death with a switch out of this world! Nicole S is a sexy woman with mad swagger and a bubble butt many women WISH they had.

Thottiana. The only BBW nominee, boasts a 58-inch bottom that you can sit a rack of BBQ ribs and a pitcher of beer on, literally!

Jazmin. This sexy sista carries around a bodacious backside that is rumored to feel like Cotton Candy."

"And Best Booty 2020 goes to..." Biscuits said before opening the envelope. "Nicole S." The crowd clapped, and every man in the building gave her a standing ovation. More so to see her walk up to the stage. Nicole S stood up and tugged her skirt down. She had on a red dress that was so tight it looked like it was painted on! It came mid-thigh and showed massive amounts of cleavage.

"Excuse me. My bad. Sorry," she said, as she squeezed by the people in her row. Her big 'ol ass couldn't help but hit several people in the face. Nicole didn't just *walk* up the stage. She *glided*. Her walk was beyond sexy. And because of her build, her hips couldn't help but swivel back and forth in figure eight-like motions. Men and women drooled watching that pretty ass walk up the aisle.

When she got to the top of the stage, she hiked her skirt up to her waist, revealing a red silk thong. She put her hands on her knees and looked over her shoulder.

"Heyyyyyyy," she said, shaking her booty enthusiastically for the crowd. That turned motherfuckers up. Hoots, hollers, whistles, and chants filled the Arena.

"Ok, ok. Let me chill. I'll turn up at the after set," Nicole said as she gasped for breath. She was handed the trophy as she looked out into the crowd. "Well, first off. I would like to thank my mom because I got my big booty from her. Thanks mom! And to all the cheese and dairy I eat, thanks for contributing to my curves. Shout out to all my ladies that were nominated. We *all* got ass. So, keep feeding those booties girls. Big butts running this shit!" Nicole said. She stuck her tongue out and twerked again before leaving the stage.

The next award went to the "#1 Thot." Trashy Treece was

the winner of that. A meth smoking, gun-toting, bi-polar thot, Trashy Treece accepted her award but was quickly "Kayne-d" by THOT Gang.

"We know muhfuckas ain't know who THOT Gang was up here. But now y'all do. And ain't no bitch in this city Thottier than us," Nadia said, taking the mike from Trashy Treece. Big Mama Drawz snatched the trophy from the frail woman's hands and pushed her down.

"Get cho skinny ass outta here hoe. You ain't no true thot," Big Mama Drawz said.

"Yeah, we'll fuck yo nigga in front of you then rob *both* y'all ass. We don't give no fucks!" Juicy said into the microphone. Juicy was a cutthroat ass gangsta bitch. A pretty ass chocolate woman who liked rough sex and was fond of armed robbery.

"Anyway, we'll take this award. And from here on out, if a THOT Gang bitch don't win this shit, we'll take it from who does," Nadia said.

"THOT Gang!" the group of women shouted before leaving the stage.

Several more awards were handed out. "Biggest Trick," "Dirtiest Fuckboy/Fuckgirl," "Most Loved Click," "Best Drip," and "#1 Rat." The last one was given by the Tattle Tellers Of America (T.T.O.A.) in another location. The rat recipient would be recorded live in a banquet hall with the other nominees and broadcast on the screens in the Expo. They weren't allowed to attend the actual ceremony, but the dumb motherfuckers accepted their nominations with pride.

There were some more hot performances and intermissions throughout the night. It was an open bar, so everyone was sipping on the best of the best and getting tipsy. Smoke from all kinds of weed filled the air in thick ghostly clouds. Brix accepted a blunt of BBC bomb from Rose.

"Tanya, the bitch that was supposed to present the next category done blacked out backstage. Dumb bitch drank too much free Patron. Anyway, I don't wanna go up there by myself. Will you come with me? We just read the shit off the teleprompter, right Rose?" Brix said and took a few deep drags from the blunt before passing it to Tanya.

"Yes Mami. You just look straight ahead. The words will be on a screen for you to read," Rose told her.

"Sure Brix, I got you," Tanya said, inhaling the strong marijuana.

"I'm gonna let my homegirl Brix give out this next honor. Ma, come on up here," Perk Thirty said. Brix stood up, and Tanya grabbed her hand. They walked to the stage together.

"This next category is a touchy one. It's one that proves loyalty is rare," Brix said. She looked at Tanya, indicating she should read the next part.

"Oh. Um, these four people give a fuck about one person and one person only. Their motherfucking *self*," Tanya said into the mic. The lights dimmed and the raspy voice returned as clips played on the screens.

"Stacey, the middle-aged bohemian who set up her best friend to go to jail, then stole her fiancé. Some say it was a plan year's in the making. Stacey claims she can't help who she fell in love with and that it "just happened."

Jerald, a boujee ex-veteran disowned his friend of twenty plus years after finding out he was homeless. Refusing to let the man who saved his life in the Army stay with him, he talked down on him instead of helping him.

Mick, the balls of steel goon who went half on a million-dollar score with his right-hand man. Only for him to run off with the $500,000 and blow it on strippers and partying. Fracturing a decades-old friendship over his dumb decision."

The screen went dark and the lights stayed dim. Brix leaned over the podium.

"The last nominee is a sneaky snake of a bitch who fucks her best friend's man behind her back. Yeah, she acts like she's all one hundred, when in fact, she's a jealous one that envies." Brix looked at Tanya and the look on her face was priceless. "Here ma, you tell the people who the winner of the Sheistyest BFF is," Brix said, opening the envelope. Tanya looked at what it said, then looked at Brix in a daze.

"What's wrong babygirl, cat got your tongue? Don't worry about it hun; I got it."

"Brix... I – "

"Give it up for Tanya y'all. I've known her since Kindergarten, and guess what? My right-hand bitch, the second in command of my click, is *fucking* my *boyfriend*. Can you believe it? Yeah, they thought I didn't know. I'm too focused on my money to notice the looks my boyfriend and best friend give each other when they think I'm not looking. The way they act weird when I enter the room like they were just doing something they shouldn't have. Tisk, tisk. It's a shame ya know? You were gonna be with me while we did big things –"

"Brix, I'm still with you. I... look. I fucked up. I'm sorry – "

"You oughta be," Brix said and pulled a knife from under the podium. She stabbed Tanya in the collarbone.

"Ahhhh!" The deceptive girl screamed.

Gutter, who felt like a deer in headlights, tried to make a run for it. The F.N.B'z , who were sitting behind him, put all sorts of weapons to his body. "Where you think you going nigga?" Someone holding a box cutter to his throat whispered in his ear. He sat back in his seat slowly.

Tanya staggered to the middle of the stage, trying to escape Brix's wrath. With each word she yelled, Brix drove the knife into another part of Tanya's body. "You...no...good...rotten... bitch! You want to be the Queen? Bitch, you're a worker bee hoe!" Brix stabbed Tanya over a dozen times. Her screams of agony echoed throughout the building. Brix rolled Tanya onto her stomach. "Since you like to stab folks in the back, let's see how *you* like it," she said, driving the Chef's knife into Tanya's shoulder blades, spinal cord, and tramp stamp. The girl lay in a pool of blood, center-stage.

Eventually, Brix got tired and threw the knife next to her former friend's butchered body. Then, she grabbed the WWS trophy and looked over at Gutter. Hate and anger filled her eyes. He recognized that look and was so scared he pissed on himself.

Tanya slowly rolled around in her own blood. She was numb and losing consciousness fast. She knew what her demise would be. She crossed her BFF because she wanted everything Brix had, and that included her man. It was an idiotic "want" that would cost her dearly. Brix stood over Tanya and bashed her skull into the stage several times with the trophy. Chunks of Tanya's skull flew into the audience. The crowd sat on the edge of their seats watching Brix bludgeon her former BFF to death.

Bucky couldn't believe what he was witnessing. If it weren't for his boys elbowing him with excitement and awe, he would've thought he was dreaming!

Breathing heavily, Brix walked back to the microphone. "Well, it looks like the Sheistyest BFF winner is unable to receive her award, so I'll accept this on her behalf and make sure it gets buried with her," Brix said, holding up the bloody trophy that had long strands of hair and flesh hanging from it. "As for you Gutter? Don't worry, I ain't gonna kill you fuckboy. I thought you were true, but you're just like every other man. And that's why I don't blame you boo. You're just being the dog ass nigga that you are. It's in your DNA. A bitch throw some pussy at you, and you're gonna hump it. I know how the game goes," Brix said, shaking her head.

Becky was right. The fuckery only got more treacherous as time went by. She sensed something wasn't right with her man and best friend. After bringing her suspicions to Rose, video footage of Gutter and Tanya having sex in various places, on various occasions, was shown to a heartbroken Brix. Those images changed her, made her *colder*. Turned her into a pure savage!

"Gutter, you will be allowed to live on one condition," Brix said. "You are no longer my dude. *Obviously*. But you *can* be a part of the Fuck Nigga Boyz and continue on in your Fuck Nigga ways. They will welcome you with open arms, so if you're willing to embrace your new life here with them, I will spare your life."

Gutter looked around the auditorium. All eyes were on him, beads of sweat coated his face as nervousness and paranoia turned into the bubble guts. He was scared shitless because he knew how Brix got down. Hell, the first night he met Brix, she had whooped a bitch and shoved a pool stick up her ass at a House party!

"Shiiiiid, you better say yes, my nigga. If fucking the plug's best friend ain't some fuck shit...Damn, you were the plug's *dude?* Man, I don't know what the fuck you were thinking," Perk Thirty said, shaking his head.

"Yeah man, that was some real live Fuck Nigga shit, my dude. Might as well roll with us and get it how you live now, fuck it." One of the F.N.B'z behind Gutter said.

"Dammmmmmn my nigga, did you pee on yourself?" Doobie, a F.N.B member said, leaning over Gutter's seat and sniffing him.

"Look dog, you only got two choices," Ham Samich told Gutter. "Either get down with us, or that bitch is gonna kill you my nigga. Simple as that."

Gutter knew he was telling the truth. Brix had just stabbed Tanya to death on stage at an Awards show. And what was so crazy, some big burly chicks had wrapped Tanya up in a rug and hauled her off stage like nothing ever happened.

"So, what's it gonna be Gutter?" Brix asked. "You an F.N.B, orrrrr?"

"I'll be a Fuck Nigga Boy. Brix, I'm s – "

"Save your sorry's nigga. You sorry alright. A sorry excuse for a man," Brix told him. "But like I said, I don't fault you. You just wanted a nut. *She,* wanted my spot. Your betrayal doesn't deserve death...yet. I don't know what a bitch gotta do to keep some loyal motherfuckers on the team, but damn! You'll fit right in with your new crew. I hope it was worth it."

The F.N.B'z congratulated him on joining their family. There were pats on the back, handshakes, daps were given, and pictures of Gutter with his new click were taken.

"Dog, you's an animal. That bitch got bricks of loud and you crept on her with her BFF? Yeah, you's a Fuck Nigga for real fam. That's what's up," Crunchy, a F.N.B member said.

Brix headed backstage to change her dress. She brought a matching one with her in case she got something on hers. In this case, it just so happened to be her former best friends' blood.

The next two presenters were a couple of UW-Eau Claire students who were also aspiring comedians. Ryan, a tall slim white guy with shaggy brown hair, and Andy, a short blonde buff dude who played football and kicks ass in Beer-Pong, approached the podium.

"What's uuuuuuup my cracka?!" Andy said into the mike.

"Shit, my honky. What it do?" Ryan said.

"Well, we're about to give out the funniest award of the night my Cracka," Andy said.

"Honky, is you talking about the blackest whiteboy of the year award?" Ryan said.

"Hell to the yeah my honky. These four dudes are one thousand percent white, but um, for some reason, they think they're black," Andy said. The crowd laughed.

"Without further ado, let's meet these doucheb – uh, I mean dudes... Chad Reynolds. This white guy says he doesn't like white people, has a Native American wife, and only drives Cadillacs," Ryan said.

"Dustin Blanderson. The ex-redneck who fell in love with Hip-Hop culture after being introduced to Tech N9ne's music a few years ago. He now rocks dreadlocks and is known to say 'GangGang' just wayyyyy too much."

"Our third wanna-be black white boy is Ty-Ty. The tall, handsome business owner is quite popular with the ladies because of his swag and sex appeal. But his constant use of the N-word, and unnecessary face tattoos got him nominated for this award," Ryan said.

"The last nominee isn't from around these parts. But his antics are so well-known across the Midwest, that his street fame earned him a blackest whiteboy nomination. Bucky, founder and leader of Pill Mobb, is still rocking the style of 90's rap stars." Andy said.

"Yeah man, you been watching that Wu-Tang show on Hulu too much my honky," Ryan told Bucky. People laughed while the trophy girl brought the envelope and trophy to the podium. Brix was just getting back to her seat when they announced the winner.

"Bucky!" Ryan and Andy shouted in unison. Bucky looked around confused. People clapped as the spotlight landed on him.

"Oh my God Daddy, you won! Go up there my nigga. Rep for Pill Mobb." GG told him and planted a kiss on his thin lips.

"Get your motherfucking ass up there and accept your award Bucky," Brix ordered him. Seeing how she just got down on Tanya, he wasn't gonna tell her no.

He stood up and jogged to the stage. He tripped on the first stair and fell on his face because his pants were so baggy. The crowd laughed at his goofy ass. The comedians handed Bucky the coveted award, and he cautiously stepped to the microphone.

"Uhhh, well, I really don't...shit bro. I don't know what the fuck to say," Bucky began, looking at the odd trophy. "This shit is nuts my nig – um...fuck! Look, I got plenty of love for black people. My girlfriend is black y'all. I – "

"Boooooooo!" the crowd grew impatient and rowdy at his stuttering and lack of a decent acceptance speech. They started throwing food and bottles at the stage.

"Wait. I, I wanna say love to my niggas Pill Mobb. We gonna keep doing it stupid big. And I um, I'm gonna keep running up a check and chasing that bag on y'all ass," Bucky said as he bobbed and weaved the flying objects coming his way. "Pill Mobb bitch!" He shouted and ran off the stage hugging the trophy to his chest.

"That whiteboy ran off the stage like he was a fugitive from justice!" Perk Thirty said and laughed. "I think – "

"Ayyyee!" A skinny white dude screamed as he ran on stage. He wore black Doc Marten boots and some tighty whitey's. That was *all.* **Black Lives Matter** was painted across his pale chest. He snatched the microphone out of Perk Thirty's hand and went on a rant.

"Fuck anyone who's racist! You bigoted motherfuckers are no better than the next person," he said and pulled a straight razor out of his underwear. Perk Thirty stepped back, and the crowd gasped. "I will die for this shit. Black Lives Matter mom. Fuck the police!" he yelled and began slicing his wrists. "Ride or die. I'll die for the cause! Ride or diiiiiiiie." Blood squirted from his sliced arteries like water fountains. He passed out and collapsed. On his way down, he hit his head on the corner of the podium. This caused another wound to open up, this time above his eyebrow. His body twitched on the ground. Perk Thirty kicked the dude's leg out of the way and stepped over him.

"Somebody come see if this crazy muthafucka dead. Damn, all crashing my gig and shit. Aight, black power, black lives matter, all that good stuff." Perk Thirty said, looking on as the white protester was hauled off on a stretcher.

"Damn y'all, this year's awards did *not* disappoint. It went down in this bitch! But we still have one more trophy to hand out. The most important honor of the night goes to the Hu$tler Of The Year. This is the man *or* woman that handled they B.I. accordingly. The true definition of a hustler is a muthafucka who doesn't sleep cuz he ain't trying to miss a single dollar. A grinding ass Go-Getter who has the leadership qualities to run an empire and put others on. This year's nominees are..."

"Papi Spice. This multi-faceted Puerto-Rican hustler travels city to city and state to state, securing the bag and living it up in the process.

Dog Food. Named after the product he moves in abundance. This heartless hustler is a favorite with the fentanyl loving Heroin addicts. Even tho they OD at an alarming rate, it hasn't stopped Dog Food's pockets from getting fatter.

Kathy. Not only does she run daycares, assisted living centers, and a recording studio, but she also has the best coke and molly money can buy.

Black. The ruthless hustler who robs his rivals and dares them to snitch. He and his Black Boy Gang move a lot of weight for good prices."

"ALRIGHT Y'ALL. This is the moment we've all been waiting for. The top honor of the night goes to..." Perk Thirty opened the envelope. "Papi Spice. Come on up fam." The whole place got to their feet and cheered for the Hu$tler Of The Year. Confetti rained down from the ceiling.

Papi Spice stood up and buttoned his sport coat. He gave his woman a kiss and pat on the butt before he strode to the stage. The beautiful trophy girl handed Papi Spice his award.

"Yo, this is crazy. Everybody knows I do this shit for my

family. For my team. But to receive acknowledgement from the streets? Yo, that's love. I was in a cell a few years ago. But I made a plan in that bitch. Cuz if you fail to plan, you plan to fail. And failure is not an option for me," Papi Spice said and pulled up his sleeve. Tattooed on his forearm was *Failure Is Not An Option*, in a freestyle script. "I'm out here bussin' moves. If y'all trying to get right, holla at cha boy. Add me on Snapchat, Papi-Spice715. I got wax, carts, weed, coke, all for the low-low. Get at me!" He said, holding the WWS award in the air. The trophy girl escorted him backstage where she proceeded to give him an honorary blowjob until completion.

"Well y'all, there you have it. Another Who Want Smoke show in the books. It keeps getting wilder and wilder each year. I can't wait to see what 2021 holds! Before y'all ride out, my boy Krispy wanna give y'all the inside scoop on the after set," Perk Thirty said. Two dark-skinned brothers with freshly trimmed beards and tapers walked on stage.

"Good lookin' fam. And don't think cuz you won best drip that you fucking in my bidness," Krispy said to Perk Thirty. "Aye, we having the after set at my crib. That's the Players Palace for those of y'all who don't know. We on sixth Ave. The crib with the big ass Lion statue out front. We got the Party Bus after this, so all you bad ass bitches feel free to join us on that muhfucka," Krispy announced into the microphone.

Tee, the other guy, was rocking red Timbs, black jeans, and a red Rock Republic shirt. His red Chicago Bulls hat was adorned with crushed red and black diamonds. "We got them beans, weed, drank...shiiiid come through and fuck wit us," Tee said.

"We players tho. No hating or fuck shit is welcome at our spot. If you not coming to turn up, get loose, smoke, drink, suck, fuck, and party like a Rockstar? Take your lame ass home then. We bout to have the Players Palace lit. No cap!" Krispy said.

"Tangy Tongue, Nicole, Pretzel Bitez... I most *definitely* wanna see y'all at the after-set," Tee said into the microphone.

"Oh, news flash muthafuckas. There will be a limited number of males allowed to enter my shit. Nothing personal fam, but um, I want to be outnumbered by *women*. Bullshit ain't nothing, too many hard legs don't make for a Players Palace in my opinion. No cap," Krispy said. "And bring your own wraps. It's the least y'all can do since we're providing the weed, damn!"

"Aight, aight, muhfucka. Go get the after-set ready," Perk Thirty said, taking over and shoo-ing Krispy and Tee off the stage. "Y'all hear that fool? Fucking in *his* bidness. Psssh. Whatever nigga, I'm drippin' like melted icicles in this bitch." Perk Thirty grabbed his award and stared at it. "Yeeeeah. Best drip muhfucka. Even the streets know." He kissed the odd trophy and raised it high in the air.

"I'm gonna take a hot shower, get super-duper fresh, and meet all the party people at fam's spot. A nigga getting his balls licked toniiiiiiiight! Thank y'all for coming out. Hope to see you next year. And hey, don't get mad if you didn't get nominated. It just means you gotta go harder next year if you wanna be on this stage. Kk? Goodnight and God bless." Perk Thirty said.

The lights in the Expo Center came on as everyone got up and stretched. Group pictures and selfies were taken against airbrushed backdrops. Phone numbers and social media handles were exchanged. Hugs, kisses, and congratulations were given. Confetti continued to sprinkle from the ceiling as more drugs and alcohol were ingested. People chit-chatted and mingled about before the place cleared out..

4

With The Shits!

"CHAUNCEY, fuck what she talking about boo, go home with me, and I will suck yo dick til you shootin' blanks!" Joy said

"Bitch, please. You can't suck no dick. Not only is my *top* off da radar, but this pussy..." Sharice paused to hike her skirt up. She didn't have on any underwear, and her shaved pussy was on full display for everyone on the Party Bus. "Will be the wettest, tightest, thang thang you've ***ever*** been in Daddy," she said, placing Chauncey's hand on her crotch.

Chauncey was a pretty boy ass player that women flocked to in droves. He was a tall, caramel-skinned brother with light brown eyes, a perfectly shaped philly fro, and lots of tattoos.

"Ho, fuck what you talking about! This nigga wit *me* tonight," Joy said, looping her arm through Chauncey's, staking her claim.

"Bitch I'll beat your –"

"Yo, yo, yo. Both of you bitches need to shut the fuck up. Y'all blowing my high, damn!"

"I'm sorry, Daddy. But you know I'm feeling you," Sharice said, batting her eyelashes.

"That's cool. But whoever getting this dick tonight gon' have to earn it!" Chauncey said.

"And how the fuck we supposed to do that?" Joy said, feeling frustrated.

"Shiiiiid, a nigga want some entertainment. Y'all gon' have to get down wit da get down. Who *really* wit da shits? I think, whoever go the hardest in a pizza fight – "

"Hell yeah dog, make them bitches pizza fight," Chauncey's friend Tone said and laughed.

"Pizza fight?" Sharice asked, looking puzzled.

"Yeah. I'm gon' get a large pizza with the works. Y'all gon' take turns slapping each other until one of you taps out, or whoever gets slapped the hardest by the time the whole pizza's gone, wins me for the night. We gon' see who really wit da shits," Chauncey said.

"Oh, hell yeah, I'm with it. You know I'm down!" Joy said.

"Girl, you better enjoy getting slapped with that pizza. Cuz that's gonna be the only *sausage* in your face tonight, cuz this dick is mine!" Sharice laughed and cupped Chauncey's crotch.

JOY JUMPED up and went straight at Sharice, but the guys at the back of the bus quickly got in between them before shit popped off.

"Chill, chill. Save all that feistiness for the pizza boxing," Chauncey said, rubbing his palms together and smiling. "Tone, call Toppers and order some shit fam."

"Yeah, and make sure it's extra cheese on that shit. This bitch wanna run her mouth, I'm filling that muthafucka up with mozzarella," Joy said. Everyone laughed.

There were close to sixty people on the 35 passenger Party Bus. Blunts were going around, and bottles were popping while people danced, talked shit, and sat on each other's laps. While Chauncey held court in the back, some other shit was going on in front.

"On da G dat hoe ass bitch bet not play with me. Ooh. That bitch don't want no smoke," Jazmin seethed.

"What is you talking about ma?" Wayne asked. He was trying to enjoy the show on the Party Bus, but Jazmin was in his ear bitching about something.

"Stankin ass Nicole. Think she da shit cuz she won best booty. Psssh, everybody know ***I*** shoulda won that shit."

Wayne looked Jazmine upside her head like she was crazy. He took a swig from his Crown Peach bottle and looked towards the back of the bus. More than forty sexy women were taking turns twerking on a glow in the dark stripper pole. Chicks were doing the splits in the aisle, pouring liquor down each other's throats, sixty-nine-ing in bikinis on top of the bar, and in the midst of all that beautiful chaos sat Nicole, (a thick ass woman shaped like the number eight). Not only were her curves au natural, but her booty was a magnificent piece of art. It moved like ocean waves at a desert rave.

"Look Jaz; you got a fat ass. No doubt, that thang you got back there is niiiice," Wayne said. "But Best Booty factors in not only size but the way it moves. The way the cheeks cup the back thigh when you stand up straight. Can we see that ass from the front? You know you're strapped when I can see you from the front and can tell you have a big ass. And how is it shaped? It's plenty of 'big butts' out there, but that don't mean they shaped the best. Is it meaty? Bubbly? Slope-ish? Wet bag of baked potato-ish? Some have that pear shape which is great. Like yours, you got that pear ass Jaz. But your walk doesn't accentuate your *ass*ets."

"Nigga, what is you talking about? I ain't trying to hear all them big ass words and shit. Aspeenchiate – "

"Accentuate," Wayne corrected her. "Anyway, that ain't the point ya dumb ass broad. Do you not see how Nicole walks? The bitch moves like a Jaguar, or a Salsa dancing Cheetah or some shit! The way her hips swivel in that rocking motion makes her ass move...I don't know, fluidly? Is Ocean-y a word? Whatever it is, that shit is sexy as a muthafucka! So, until you can get your ass to move with some *mmpf* while you walk, you ain't got nothing on that bitch," Wayne said and pointed at Nicole.

Nicole danced in her seat, slapped girls on their twerking butts, and took pics with her WWS Award. The bitch deserved to win alright. Everybody and they mama knew Nicole was winning that shit. Jazmine's hating ass just didn't want to accept reality. But Wayne was about to spit the real to her.

"Look ma. You see that shit going on with Chauncey? That nigga always got hoes fighting over him. Shit's crazy! But I ain't hating. Fam a player. 'Ol pretty ass nikkuh. Bitches love that muthafucka. You don't see me like 'that ho ass nigga ain't shit. He a mog' and all that do you? Hell naw. Hating ain't in my blood, and it's really not a good look for you ma,"

"Shut the fuck up nigga. Ain't nobody hating," Jazmin said.

"Bitch, yes you is. All in yo feelings cuz Nicole won. So what? Her winning doesn't take away from the fact that you still have a *great* ass. Shit, brush that loss off. Ain't no thang. Congratulate, but never hate babygirl. Shit, Joy and Sharice bad as a muthafucka. Ain't a nigga on this bus that wouldn't hit them. But they trying to smash Chauncey and ready to throw hands to have him. Now, I ain't the ugliest dude in the world, but damn, bitches don't fight over me like that! This nigga got dimes throwing themselves at him every day all day. I just tip my hat to the nigga and tell him to do his thang. Why would I hate that brother for what God blessed him with? Why would I call him out his name just because some people like him more than me? Ya see, hate breeds envy, jealousy, and all kinds of spiteful emotions. Let's reverse the roles. If you had won, how would you feel if the other nominees were ice grilling you or talking down on you?" Wayne asked.

"Shiiiit, I wouldn't give a fuck. Muhfuckas can kiss my ass," Jazmin said.

"Exactly! Cuz you ain't do shit but do you and win an award right? So, if a muthafucka's hating, it's cuz they have their *own* issues that has nothing to do with you," he told her. Jazmin sat and pondered on what Wayne said. She really wasn't trying to hear that shit, but he was keeping it 100 with her and breaking it down in a way that made sense.

"I feel you. But I still don't like the bitch," Jazmin said.

"Yeah, well that's your problem. Quit worrying about that bitch and go show them hoes how a real big booty gets down on the pole," he encouraged her.

"Boy, shut up. You just wanna see my ass."

"Duh, hell yeah I do! I wanna see that thang jiggle on the pole," Wayne said, smiling. Just then, a bunch of people shouted "heyyyy" and cheered on Nicole as she stood up and twerked her fabulous butt on the pole. Wayne smiled even bigger because he *knew* what was about to happen.

"Uh-uh. No this bitch didn't! Hold my purse, Wayne. I'm finna show this ho what time it is," Jazmin said, standing up and handing her handbag to Wayne. Gucci Mane and Megan Thee Stallion's *"Big Booty"* was bumping as she made her way towards the back.

"Go Nicole! Go Nicole! Go Nicole!" The chants went as she broke it down, throwing her cheeks from side to side. You could tell she was basking in the moment, eating up her fifteen minutes of fame, because she was oblivious to Jazmin creeping up.

"Uh oh, I think we have a challenger ladies and gentlemen,"

Krispy announced as he walked up on Jazmin, licking his lips and looking her up and down. She squeezed by Krispy, making sure to rub her butt against him as she walked by.

Nicole looked over her shoulder at Jazmin. She knew wasn't nobody fucking in her business, so she turnt up even more. "Krispy, gimme some of that Hen Daddy," Nicole said. He hurried up and went over to her. Nicole opened her mouth and threw her head back. Her purple tongue ring sparkled under all the neon strobe lights. Krispy filled her mouth with Hennessey, and she chugged it down to chants of "drink, drink, drink!"

Jazmin was tired of Nicole getting all the damn shine. She stood next to Nicole and grabbed the stripper pole with one hand. There is something about a woman looking back at her own booty while she shakes it, that makes the visual even more spectacular. As "new booty on the scene," Jazmin arched her back and began a sea of bootylicious waves for all eyes to see. Ripples of lust wobbled beneath her skin like a flag blowing in the windy city.

"Ok, ok. We got a twerk-off y'all," a man named Cam announced. Everyone on the bus gathered around the pole and watched the festivities. Jazmin was wearing a skin-tight dress that barely covered her butt cheeks. She didn't give a fuck that the purple fabric rose up to her hips, exposing her full moon while she shook what her mama gave her.

Taken off guard by the runner-up of best booty, Nicole was determined to show this bitch why *she* was chosen for the award. "Hey, let me hit that Peach Crown," she told Wayne. He got up and handed her the orange Crown Royal bag with the half-drunken bottle in it. Jazmin twisted the cap off and took three big gulps before passing it back to Wayne. "Good looking Daddy," she said and winked at him.

People were Facebook Live, and Snapchatting Jazmin go ham on the pole. Cellphones were held inches from her ass while they recorded the beautiful redbones skills. Never a hater, Nicole let the girl do her thing, nodding in approval to some of her moves. But she was not about to let her steal the spotlight though.

"Someone put some shit on that I can get loose to," Nicole said. Krispy's brother Mario was in charge of the music. He tapped the screen on his phone, and "*Money*" by Cardi B came roaring from the surround sound speakers.

"Ayyyye!" Women shouted upon hearing the familiar beat drop. Nicole stuck her tongue out and hiked her dress up. Just about anyone with a fat ass looks good shaking it, but the ones that can make their butts do "tricks" are in a league of their own!

Nicole flexed her glute muscles, making each cheek bounce up and down in tune with the beat. Her ass looked like a 6-4 hitting switches in a West coast rap video. The more the bus cheered her on, the harder she went. But just as she was getting into a zone, the music cut off.

"Hey!" "What the fuck yo?" "What happened to the music?" People shouted.

"Yo, calm the fuck down," Cam said, standing in his seat. With one hand on the mirrored ceiling to maintain his balance, he addressed the bus. "I got five muthafuckin' bands for the best twerker," he said, pulling a wad of cash out of his pocket. Bitches stood up, raised their hands and began shaking ass like it was no tomorrow.

"No, no, no, you thirsty ass bitches! I wanna see these two and these two *only* go at it," Cam said, pointing to Nicole and Jazmin. "This nigga Chauncey got hoes finna Pizza fight over his ass. Well, I want a twerk-off goddamnit!"

"Hell yeah, my nigga. That's what's up. No cap! Let's get this shit cracking," Krispy said.

"Yo, this how we gon' do this. Wayne, Belinda, Krispy, and Mario, y'all judge the competition. Y'all some 100 muthafuckas, so I know y'all will be fair. I ain't gonna pick cuz I'm putting the money up, so I'll stay out of it and just enjoy the show," Cam said.

"I think we should both pick a song to twerk too. And whoever has the best moves during the entire song should get the five G's," Jazmin said.

Cam nodded in agreement. "I'm with that ma. Sounds good to me. Nicole, you in?"

"Hell yeah I'm in nigga. The holidays are coming up, I can use them five bands," Nicole said, rubbing her palms together.

"Aight, it's settled then. Light some blunts y'all. And whatever you ladies need to get loose... make it happen," Cam told them.

Nicole and Jazmin each poured shots of their choice drink and took pulls from the marijuana blunts being passed around. Nicole stood up, cracked her knuckles and did stretches.

"Bitch, I don't know what you think you doing. You finna run a marathon or something?" Jazmin commented and laughed. A few other people laughed as well.

"Yeah, I'm about to run alright. Run up this $5,000 bag I'm bout to get on your ass!"

"Psssh, whatever. So, what's up Daddy? We gon' get this shit shaking or what?" Jazmin asked Cam.

"Babygirl, *you* da one finna do the shaking. So, whenever you ready, pick your song and get to shaking that shiiiiiiit," Cam said, and hit the blunt.

Jazmin chose French Montana's "*Pop That*" as her song. By the time Rozay said, *drop that pussy bitch,* the second time, she was going in, hands on her knees, popping her ass like wheelies at X Games. Even though she wasn't a stripper, she used the pole like a pro, doing some quite impressive moves that made her audience "ooh." The five-minute song was the perfect soundtrack to her booty-shaking extravaganza. When it was over, she put one hand on her hip and breathed heavily. People stood up and cheered loudly for her performance.

Nicole's song of choice was the one she won her High School talent show to, "*Drop It Low*" by Ester Dean. It was an oldie but goodie for her because she had a sick routine to it. She slung her buttocks like a boomerang and held nothing back. When she made her cheeks clap to the beat, everyone on the bus joined in by clapping their hands enthusiastically. She knew how to contract her butt muscles and make them bounce up and down too, but since Jazmin incorporated that in her routine, Nicole decided against it.

What she did do was raise one leg above her head, resting her heel on the pole, while her hips gyrated perfectly to the beat. Her pussy lips popped out of her thong, and that got the men hyped up. Camera flashes went off and tongues wagged thirstily. She saved her most exciting moves for the final one minute and three seconds of the song. She dropped into the splits position and made her pussy lips kiss the floor. Everyone stood in their seats and cheered her on. Their encouragement provoked her to do a headstand. She used her ankles to hold on to the pole while she rested on her hands and head, twerking like there was no tomorrow.

Feeling outdone, Jazmin also dropped down into the splits. Turning things up a notch, she pulled her titties out and sucked on her own nipples! That got some loud applause from the guys. Someone popped a bottle of Champagne and sprayed the two women with cool bubbly. Mario played a third song for the women.

"*Big Money*" by Milwaukee's own Munch Lauren made the whole Party Bus go nuts! The two women turned their backs to each other and went all in. Their big booties bounced against each other like they were slap boxing. It was a beautiful sight to see those round things collide passionately back and forth.

There was no holding back as they booty bumped each other and went cheek for cheek.

"Hey! Hey! Hey! Hey!" The overcrowded bus was rocking with chants and hard-hitting bass. A few women watching the twerk off were so into it, they made it rain. Dollar bills and more champagne rained down on Jazmin and Nicole until the song ended.

"Hell muthafuckin' yeah!" Cam shouted. "That was worth five geez if you ask me. Give these two ladies a round of applause y'all. Come on now, give it up for them." The Bus rocked with applause, whistles, and mad love for the two twerkers. "Alright, alright, calm down y'all. It's time to pick the winner. Judges..."

"Shiiiiid, that was off the muthafuckin' radar y'all! Damn. I think you both japped the fuck out, but I'm picking Jazmin," Wayne said. Half the bus clapped and whistled for his pick.

"What? Man, you trippin' dog. Nicole's my pick. She spazzed out in a headstand my nigga. Nicole, you did that ma. No cap," Krispy said. The other half clapped for his pick.

"Belinda, who's your pic baby girl?" Cam asked.

"Damn, I ain't know it would be this hard – "

"That's what *she* said," Wayne joked.

"Boy, shut your nasty self up. I gotta agree with Krispy's pick tho. Nicole showed out," Belinda said.

"Aight. That's two to one for Nicole. Mario, it's on you dog. If you pick Nicole, she's the five bands winner. If you're riding with Jazmin, we gonna have to have someone do the tie breaker."

Those that knew Mario best knew he had a thing for redbones, so it was no surprise to everyone when he said Jazmin's name.

"Ohhhhhhh," Cam said, counting the five geez one more time. "Well, it looks like we got a tie y'all. We need a neutral muthafucka to pick the winner fairly. Fam, what's your name bro?" he asked a stocky dude sipping a Corona.

"Who, me? I'm Bruce."

"Ok Bruce. You wanna pick the winner, my guy?" Cam asked.

"Yeah man, why not? They both did they muthafuckin' thang if you ask me. But shit, I gotta go with Nicole. Shorty da truth," Bruce said, eyeing Nicole hungrily. She smiled at him and blew him a kiss.

"Bullshit!" Jazmin spat and stomped off to the front of the bus, salty as hell. She'd lost twice in one night to the bitch. She was heated!

Everyone cheered for the winner. Cam handed Nicole her prize money, and she smiled from ear to ear. She thanked everyone for the love and crowd participation that fueled her adrenaline. Then she took pics with the money next to her trophy. Wayne went back up front to calm Jazmin down, but she wasn't hearing none of it. She was steaming mad, so he gave her some space and mingled with the other passengers.

The music came back on and the party resumed. The Party Bus pulled into the Bowl Winkle's parking lot and Tone hopped off to grab the Pizzas from Toppers. By this time, everyone on the bus was high and/or drunk. The next act would be a stoner's comedic dream come true.

Tone returned with ten large pizzas. He handed Chauncey the top box, and the other ones were passed around the bus.

"Yeeeeah, a Meat Topper tallboy," Chauncey said, opening the box. Steam rose from the delicious looking pizza loaded with meat and plenty of cheese. "Alright, this is how this is gonna go. Y'all gonna rock paper scissors to see who goes first. It's eight slices here. You can hit your opponent however you wish, but it has to be with the pizza. Be sure you throw it hard tho, cuz if nobody taps out by slice eight, the winner will be whoever went the hardest," Chauncey said, looking back and forth between Joy and Sharice. "Any questions?"

They both shook their heads no, and everyone on the bus got their phones out. Chauncey had Joy sit across from Sharice, so they'd be face to face. They both sat on the edge of their seats until their knees were almost touching. Chauncey sat next to Sharice with the open pizza box on his lap. Joy won the best out of three rock paper scissors, so she got to go first.

Chauncey extended the pizza box to Joy, and she took out the first slice. Strings of melted cheese hung from the pizza as she smiled and jumped at Sharice. She flinched, causing people to laugh. "Scary ass ho, whatchu jumpin' foe?"

"Whatever bitch. Just – "

SMACK! Joy caught her while she was still talking. A piece of pepperoni was stuck to Sharice's cheek as Joy threw the used slice in the top part of the pizza box. Sharice grabbed a slice and positioned it so that the whole slice rested in her palm. **SMACK!** She put some force behind hers, and because she palmed it, her slap was harder. Joy held her first piece by the crust end, but after feeling Sharice's slap, she decided to do it that way too. "How dat feel bitch?" Joy smirked and threw her second slice in the box. Cheese and Pizza sauce slid down Sharice's cheek. "Ooooooh" and "Dammmmmn" were the familiar responses echoing on the Party bus.

When Sharice slapped Joy with the next piece, it stung her hand and caused tomato sauce to ricochet on Sharice. Joy felt it so much that it ignited something within her. She shook off the sting and reached for her next slice. Making a show of things, she took a bite of the cheesy pizza and moaned erotically. **SMACK!**

While chewing, she cold-clocked Sharice across the nose with the palmed pizza. Joy was able to catch her from ear to ear, snapping Sharice's head back like she got whiplash!

"Yo, you ok ma? You can tap out," Chauncey told Sharice.

"Fuck is you saying nigga? Ain't no quitter in my blood," Sharice said, regaining her composure as she blinked rapidly and shook off Joy's last hit. Sharice was dizzy, so her next blow didn't resonate well. But Joy came harder and stronger with each turn. By the time the pizza was gone, Sharice was seeing threes and her head was leaning to one side. Covered in cheese, meat and sauce the women nodded at each other while Chauncey announced the clear winner.

"Joy, you put it down. You wit the shits for real," he said, raising Joy's arm in the air.

"Muthafuckin right I'm wit the shits!" Joy said, smiling big and sitting on Chauncey's lap. He cleaned her up and tongued her down. The two molested each other's bodies with pure lust and desire in front of everyone.

"My nigga, I know you were the tie-breaker judge, but I just can't honor your decision," Jazmin said, as she walked up to Bruce.

Bruce was chugging thirstily from a Corona bottle like he never had beer before.

"Hey nigga, you hear me talking to you?" Jazmin said.

"Huh? You talking to me baby? What's up?"

"Yeah, you bald-headed, pink lip muthafucka. I'm talking to your bitch ass. You picked that hoe over me? Ho ass nigga, ***I'm*** that bitch..." Jazmin went on a rampage and verbally assaulted Bruce with the kick of a Draco.

"Look at yo dusty, dirty, po' ass. What the fuck is you wearing dude? You get that shit off a bum in my alley or something? Wait, that's old man Hubbard's shirt. You better give that old wino back his shit man. Broke ass nigga. Lame ass nigga. 'Ol dick in da booty ass nigga! Pussy ass nigga. Do you even *get* pussy? This the most pussy you done seen in yo life ain't it?" Jazmin said, pointing around at the half-naked or completely nude women on the Party Bus. "Talking like ***I*** ain't that bitch. Bitch ass nigga –"

"Look hoe. I ain't finna be no mo bitch ass nig –"

"Bitch...ass...nigga...*PLEASE!*" Jazmin shouted in his face. Bruce laughed and finished the rest of his beer. He even made a show of it by tilting the bottle up and letting the last suds drip slowly out. He smacked his lips as he savored the frothy beer on his tongue.

"This bitch funny as a muthafucka ain't she y'all?" he said to the people sitting around him. **WHAP!** Without warning, Bruce cracked the Corona bottle across her temple. Shards of glass sprinkled everywhere, causing him to flinch back. Lucky for him, because Jazmin reacted immediately upon getting hit with the beer bottle. She swung a round house right and hit nothing but air. Realizing this bitch wanted to fight, Bruce grabbed her by the throat and head-butted her.

Jazmin staggered back and grabbed the stripper pole to catch her balance. She touched her bloody forehead then looked at her hand. "Nigga, did you just head-butt me?" she asked, stunned. Jazmin took her heels off and everybody got geeked.

"Aww shit dog, she done came up out the shoes. It's on now!" someone shouted.

Jazmin was from the hood. She grew up with five brothers. Three were still alive and two of them were locked up. She was taught to be tough, hard, and aggressive because that was what the climate called for in the Jungle. So, while she was *all* woman, Jazmin went harder than most *men* did.

She rained a fury of fists and slaps on Bruce's face and head. Like a man possessed, he welcomed her assault and didn't even try to dodge her blows.

"Come on bitch. Bring it! Yeah, hit me harder hoe," Bruce said. His taunting puzzled her, and she stepped back. Bruce picked up where she left off. "Come on ho. This is how you do it," Bruce yelled, punching himself in the face and head. "Why you stop? You can't hang bitch?" Bruce was slapping and punching himself very hard while he taunted Jazmin.

She couldn't believe what he was doing. She stood there with her hands on her hips and her mouth wide open. *This nigga crazy ass a muthafucka. Retarded ass fool,* she thought to herself. People on the bus were laughing, instigating, rooting for who they wanted to win, and taking pics and video of what was going on. But one thing they didn't do was intervene. They didn't want no smoke by getting caught in the middle of the drama.

"You know what, I can't be playing with you," Jazmin walked back to her seat and sat down. People thought she was surrendering until she pulled a Smith & Wesson out of her purse. ***Rarr!*** "Bitch" ***Rarr!*** "Ass" ***Rarr!*** "Nigga. I ain't finna be boxing with yo retarded strength ass. That lead take care of my biz," Jazmin said and kissed the still smoking barrel of her .38 Special.

She shot him twice in the chest and once in the face. His head exploded like a water balloon getting thrown off a roof. Bruce's brains and blood splattered on the windows and people sitting by him. They inched away slowly when Jazmin began shooting, hoping and praying she'd feel better once Bruce was dead. They were all trying to make it back home the same way they left. Poor Bruce though, the only place he was going was to the morgue.

"What the fuck Jaz?! you done popped this nigga on the Bus," Krispy said, stepping over Bruce's dead body.

"Shiiiid, so what? Nigga shouldn't have put his hands on me; he'd still be alive. Bitch made muthafucka thought it was sweet."

"Girl, you crazy as a muthafucka. Sit yo ass down and put that pistol up," Wayne told her, wrapping his arms around Jazmin's shoulders and leading her back to her seat.

"I told that bitch ass nigga don't play wit me. That's what he get." Jazmin said and slipped the chrome gun back into her purse. She pulled a wad of money out of her purse and walked back to where she shot Bruce at. "My bad if I got that fuck nigga's blood on y'all," she said, handing out money for them to buy new fits with since she ruined theirs when she shot Bruce. They all graciously accepted her money and apology but didn't *dare* say a slick thing about shit! The music kept playing and everyone resumed dancing and kicking it like a homicide didn't just take place. The BBC elbowed each other.

"Giiiirl, are you thinking what I'm thinking?" Summer asked her click. Rose and GG looked at each other knowingly.

"TLB," they said in unison. Jazmin had just murdered a dude in cold blood, then walked back to her seat like it was nothing. A heartless killer who didn't give a fuck and would body a motherfucker anywhere, any time. Jazmin had *Tryfe Lyfe Bitch* written all over her, and the BBC was gonna make sure she got on the team.

"We'll let 'ol girl calm down before we holler at her tho," Rose said.

"Yeah, no use running up on the bitch after she done put holes in a nigga. Give her some space for a minute," GG said. The girls nodded in agreement.

The bus driver was told to pull into an alley, where a few guys on the bus disposed of Bruce's body in a garbage dumpster. Everyone on the bus had seen people get shot or worse before, so there was no screaming or scattering like roaches with the lights on once Jazmin started bussin'. But everyone did keep a close eye on her.

Even though people were allowed their weapons after the awards, they were on some have fun, kick it, and chill shit. Damn near everybody on the bus was strapped but didn't need a weapon, except Bruce obviously. That was *his* bad.

5

The After-$et

"BITCH, you just braided his hair this morning, I'm braiding his shit now. Fuck whatchu talking about!" A beautiful Mexican woman exclaimed.

At Krispy's bachelor pad, an intense spade game was going on in the kitchen. CJ was sitting at said game, trying to get his last book. A sexy ass Mexican chick was standing behind CJ parting his hair. Two minutes prior, an Asian model went to get some grease to do the pretty boys mountain of beautiful hair. It was thick, black, and sexy, (like a bad southern chick). But by the time she got back with the grease, 'ol girl was already playing in his hair.

"Thirsty ass bitch, go ahead," the Asian model surrendered and walked away. She didn't want no smoke with the heavily pierced and tatted Mamacita. It was like that with CJ though. He kept his hair long so that he could have a different beautiful woman braid his hair every day. He had designer cornrows for the Awards but took them down after the show. Now he was gonna let whoever wanted to do his shit do it, while he tried to win some bread at the Spades table.

"Damn fam, y'all bitches down here bad as a muhfucka, and they *choosing*. First the pizza slapping hoes, now it's some hair braiding jump-offs? Mannnnn, it goes down in the EC!" Cam said, getting a beer out of the fridge. Cam was from Detroit, a real live city built on blood, sweat, tears, and hustle. But after witnessing how stomp down these bitches were over their territory (men, accolades, popularity), he came to the realization that it was gangsta shit going down even in small towns. Cam flew down to attend the Awards and fuck with his boy Wayne.

"Yeah my nigga, that's what I been trying to tell y'all all along. I said the same thing after I first got here. These muthafuckas bout that life too, and the bread good as a *bitch* fam. That's the most important thang. But yeah, they funny as a bitch ain't they?" Wayne said and laughed. Cam laughed with him and they shook up. They were standing in the back yard watching two chicks wrestle in an inflatable kiddie pool full of coleslaw.

"I mean, look at this shit. Bad bitches wrestling in pudding – "

"Uh, fam. I don't think that's pudding. That's..." Wayne walked up to the pool and dipped his hand inside it. The creamy white side-dish clung to his finger. "Coleslaw my nigga."

"Whaaaat? Dam, yo. These hoes wrestling in *coleslaw*?" Cam laughed hard. "This shit wild as fuck dog."

It was like that at Krispy's after-sets. You never knew what you might see at his spot. It was nothing for you to see midget sword-swallowers, topless mermaids in the jacuzzi, head-stand beer keg chugging contests. On any given night, any of those things could be popping off at his spot. But this was the honorary after-set for the Who Want Smoke Awards. He had to do it big and get creative on 'em. So, there was a wrestling competition held in a 12-foot pool full of coleslaw in the backyard. Topless waitresses on roller skates passed out flaming cocktails to all the guests. Naked Twister was going on in the Den where on-lookers and new-aged hippies smoked weed out of a penis bong and did Jello Shots out of syringes.

Krispy showed GG, Summer, and Rose, around his place. They were quite impressed with how he had everything set up.

"You put together all these themes?" Rose asked.

"Yeah, me and my boy Tee be playing the game, smoking weed, and thinking of new shit to do at the spot. We try to do something different every rip. Wild ass shit that be having social media buzzing," Krispy said.

"That's what's up. You have a nice place, and I love all of the themes. You remind me of a young Diddy," Summer said.

"Thanks, baby girl. Does that mean you gon' give a nigga some fucking with?"

"Um, no. You cute, but you can't handle all this baby," Summer replied.

"Hmpf, whatever girl. I can handle anything you throw my way!"

Summer patted him on his cheek. "Sure you can boo. Sure you can. But for real, you should think about getting into party planning or event hosting. You have dope ideas."

"Somebody else told me that before, but I don't know," Krispy admitted.

"Damn, what are those, caramels?" Rose asked, pointing at a silver platter piled with a four-foot-tall pyramid display of light brown cubes.

"Nah, those are Dabs," Krispy said. Just then, a short flamboyantly dressed man walked up to them. "Tell 'em what cha got there dog."

"Hi ladies, I am the creator of these *fiiiiine* treats you're looking at," he said, picking up a few cubes and holding them in his open palm. "I'm Dab Daddy, and these are my trademark Dab cubes."

"Dab Daddy?" Summer asked, scrunching up her face.

"That's my name. Please wear it out," he said and laughed.

"Nigga, who you think you is, a pimped-out version of the Migos?" GG said. *"Dab Daddy"* was a banging ass Migos track that came out in 2015. The man in front of them wore a neon green sequin three-piece suit with a matching Fedora. The entire get-up had him looking like one of Kat Williams' characters.

"Haha, funny Chocolate Thunder," he clapped back. "Them niggas wish they was as fly as me. And no, I'm no rapper carbon copy. I am origin-*AL*," he said, brushing his shoulders off and stroking his goatee. His two front teeth were gold and had a diamond-encrusted D on each of them. He smiled from ear to ear and they shone brightly.

"Whatever Money Mike. Whatcha got there?" Rose asked.

"Well, y'all know what wax dabs are right?"

"That's wax? Them muthafuckas look like them little caramel candies you eat," GG said.

"I know right?" Dab Daddy chuckled. "That's the appeal Chocolate Thunder. They look like candy, and they're sweet as a bitch! These are pure honeycomb dabs. Hundred dollars a cube." He explained his creation of the butane hash oil poured over marijuana to the women. The THC from the plant material dissolved into the butane, and is then pressed through a filter, which forms a gummy-like substance. Dab Daddy used the highest quality Sativas (which are the energetic species of Marijuana plants), to make the Dab cubes in question.

"Damn, my nigga. I don't know all that Scientific mumbo-jumbo you just said, but whatever you do to whip these muhfuckas up, they fire! No cap," Krispy said.

"You don't look like no lab Scientist to me," Rose commented.

"Looks can be deceiving ma. Don't let the drip fool you. I'm a beast with this shit."

"Shiiiid, let us see what it do then," Summer said. There were glass "dab rigs" on the table for people to smoke out of. Dab Daddy picked one up.

"Nah, Dab Daddy. We only smoke blunts. Can you melt some down for us?" Rose asked.

"Yeah, and pour it in here," GG said, splitting a Mango Swisher Sweet open.

"Sure ladies," Dab Daddy said, honoring their request. Once the cubes were melted down, they drizzled the sticky goo inside the wrap and filled it with BBC Bomb.

"If this shit do what it do, we're gonna make you a very wealthy man Dab Daddy," Rose told him as she lit the blunt up.

"Well, I'm doing alright financially, but I'm always open to new avenues of revenue."

"Myyyyy nigga," Summer replied.

"Come on y'all, let me finish showing y'all around the crib," Krispy said. The ladies followed him as he took them on a tour of his two-story home.

"Damn, this shit potent as a muthafucka," Rose said, choking and coughing on the dab laced blunt. She passed it to GG who also choked and coughed.

"Holy motherfucking fuck! What the hell that nigga put in this shit," GG said, her eyes watered heavily, and drool ran from the corner of her mouth.

"I don't know, but that shit gon' have you higher than Giraffe pussy! No matter what kind of weed you mix it with, his dab cubes gon' take you to the moon," Krispy said. When Summer took a hit, she turned red and drooled on the floor.

"You ok mami?" Rose asked, patting her friend on the back.

"I…I'm good. Just…need…w-water," she gasped. Krispy ran and grabbed some bottled waters and gave one to each of them.

"Yo, listen carefully when 'ol girl passes us," Krispy said, nodding to a beautiful redbone heading their way. A thick ass woman in grey leggings walked up to Krispy. Even though rap music was blasting in the living room, a different sound accompanied her.

"Nigga, you got bitches on the ceiling now? Damn, it gets wilder and wilder every time I come to your after-sets," she said.

"Hell yeah. I gotta outdo myself every rip. No cap!"

"That's what's up. What's popping downstairs?" she asked.

"Shiiiid, Tequila pong, stripper pole, a few other thangs."

"Tequila pong? For real?"

"Yeah girl, gone down there and jump in," Krispy told her.

"I think I will. A bitch trying to get *lit* tonight," she said and walked past them towards the basement. GG, Summer, Rose, and Krispy stared in awe at her backside as she walked off. Her name was Kaneetra, a big booty woman who when she walked, Conga drums played from somewhere.

"What the fuck was that sound?" GG asked Krispy and stared at the fat ass from afar.

"That's her ***ass!*** Rumor has it, she had some kind of special device implanted in her butt that plays conga drums to sync with the bounce of her butt cheeks when she walks."

"Whaaaaaaat?" GG, Summer, and Rose shouted in unison.

"Yup. Don't know how, but that shit is bananas!" Krispy exclaimed.

"Damn, you can do shit like that?" Rose asked.

"I guess so," Krispy responded and shrugged.

"Girl, it sounded like some African tribe was jamming out when that bitch walked by!" GG said. "Muthafuckas back home ain't gonna believe us when we tell them about all the shit we done seen go down tonight."

"I know right?" Summer said.

"Yeah, well y'all ain't seen shit yet. Come on," Krispy told them.

In the basement, a group of men were on their knees playing 4-5-6 for a pile of money. Lots of shit-talking was going on that amplified the game. In the corner of the basement was a stripper pole surrounded by a long maroon leather sectional. People lounged on it drinking and smoking while women took turns shaking their goods on the glow in the dark pole. Colorful strobe lights flashed to the beat of the music thumping from the entertainment system.

On the opposite side of the basement was a ping-pong table where half-naked people played "Tequila Pong."

"Fuck Beer pong. We figured Tequila would have muhfuckas *sloppy* drunk!" Krispy told BBC and laughed.

"I might have to get in a game of that later," Summer said, intrigued.

There was also a bedroom and bathroom in the basement that were both occupied. Loud, enthusiastic moans came from the opposite side of those doors.

"Somebody's in there getting it in," GG commented.

"Always," Krispy replied, walking them back upstairs. He took them up a spiral staircase that led to the second floor.

"My room is off-limits," he said, using a key to open his bedroom door. When they walked in, the women looked at each other like *WTF?!* Krispy's room looked like a 1970's Porn set!

"James, what I tell you about getting on my bed? Boy, get your ass in yo room!" Krispy yelled to the big ass German Shepard that was chilling on his circular waterbed. The dog hopped off and ran into an adjacent room. There was a bathroom that had a sliding partition leading to Krispy's walk-in closet and a small bedroom that was for his dog James.

"Welcome to the Players Habitacion," Krispy said, sweeping

his arms across the spacious master bedroom. In one corner of the room, a huge leather sex swing hung from the ceiling. A shelf full of sex toys, XXX games, lubes, condoms, and porn videos sat next to the swing. Lava lamps and LED blacklights were strategically placed throughout the room. A mechanical bull sat in another corner of the room. Krispy hopped onto his waterbed and picked up a remote. He pushed a couple of buttons and the circular bed began to rotate and vibrate slowly.

"It can spin at different speeds," he told them. The bed was in the center of the room. It had three steps that led up to it and a velvet tufted cocktail ottoman at the foot of it. A heart-shaped mirror was on the ceiling directly above the King size waterbed. A camcorder on a tripod stood in another corner, pointed directly at the bed. Krispy saw the women staring at the portrait on his wall behind the bed.

"Yeah, that's my boo," he said, smiling up at the 70 x 80 oil painting.

"Toni Braxton?" Summer questioned with raised eyebrows.

"Yup! *Un-break my hearrrrrrt. Say you'll love me again,"* Krispy sung off-key.

"Um, don't quit your day job my guy," GG said, and the girls all laughed.

"Whatever, don't be hating," he said, getting off the bed. "I gotta attend to my bash, so make y'all selves at home. You need anything, just let me know," he walked them into the hallway, and locked his door.

"Good looking Krispy. I gotta pee, I'll catch y'all downstairs," Rose told everyone. Summer and GG went in separate directions to scope out the rest of the party.

~

"I DON'T GIVE a fuck what these niggaz and bitches say. Call me a Hoe, a thot, a slut, whatever you wanna call me. I like to fuck.

So what? Shit, what's wrong with that? Niggas like to fuck! We the bitches that like to fuck that *they* fuck. Shiiiid, so muthafuckin what? They players and macks cuz they fuck a lot of women, but we get labeled the bad ones when we have sex?! Psssh, what the fuck eva. I'm a do me, and them, and him, and whoever the fuck I wanna *do,* cuz I'm a grown ass muthafuckin' woman," an animated chick said to the mini crowd surrounding her. She was a beautiful curvaceous woman in a purple dress and glittery thigh-high purple suede boots. She was holding court on the patio where Tee was barbecuing ribs, chicken, brats and burgers.

"Yo, I feel you. These bitches be acting like they ain't fucking. They having sex with they man and creeping with other niggas. Come on ma, keep that shit one hunnid. At least *you* is. I definitely respect it, but it's the label of slut, hoe, whore – "

"Cuz of *YOU* niggas!" she said, pointing at Tee.

He pulled a rack of ribs off the grill and put the fat, sizzling slab of meat in her face. "Look hoe, I already said I was wit you. But all that finger in my face shit I don't do. Pipe yo fine ass down foe I smack you wit dis hot ass rack of ribs," Tee warned her.

"My bad Daddy. I'm just trying to school these bitches. Fuck these niggaz, then ***fuck*** these niggaz...if that's what you want to do."

Her name was Purple Haze, a half Dutch, half black stunner known for bussin' down around town. Several women were lounging on lawn chairs, waiting for the food to be done. Purple Haze was trying to get the women to embrace their "inner-ho." GG happened to step out on the patio to see what that delicious smell was when Purple was talking.

"Hey what's your name ma?" GG asked.

"Purple Haze," she replied, looking GG up and down. Purple knew a Bad Bitch when she saw one and gave her a wink of acknowledgement. The same way niggas tip they hats to other bosses doing their thing.

"I'm Gushy. I couldn't help but hear your theory on having sex. *Lots* of sex."

"Yeah, I was just telling these beautiful women, there is nothing wrong with admitting your love for sex. If you like multiple dicks or the same dick, you know you like it. Keep that shit one-hunnid. Me? I like ***new*** dick. Different niggas got different moves, different sizes, different skills, different ways they talk dirty...I like the variety. I get bored easily," Purple Haze admitted.

"That's what's up ma. Trust me, I feel you. I'm the same way. Some niggas choke you while they hit it and you ain't gotta ask him too. It's just a part of his repertoire. Some niggas pull your hair and bite your neck at the same time. Yeah, I know what you mean Purple Haze," GG said. Purple Haze absentmindedly rubbed her thighs together and licked her lips at GG's declarations of getting choked and hair-pulling.

"But don't limit your variety. My eclectic tastes are not just with my sex life, but my goals and hustle too. Fucking is cool. This party shit is cool. Hell, this the most lit afterset I've ever been to, and I been to *plenty*. But is the reward worth your actions? If it is, by all means, keep doing it. If not, *make* it worth it," GG said.

"That's what I been trying to tell these chicks," Tee said. "All dis money out here–"

"My nigga, I hear you and all that, but whatever you got on that grill done invaded a bitch nostrils from *inside* the crib and gave me a nosegasm! I came out here to eat and done ran into some real shit getting shared." GG shook her head and held a paper plate in front of her. "So, can I taste yo meat Daddy?"

Tee took one look at that chocolate Goddess and filled her plate with every piece of meat he could. GG walked back in the house with Chicken, brats, ribs, and a burger.

"Got another one for THOT Gang," GG announced, holding the plate out to Summer and Rose. She was chewing on a drumstick while she said it.

"Guuuuuurl, that shit looks fire!" Summer said grabbing a brat.

"It is," GG mumbled, her mouth full of chicken,

"What's that about a new THOT?" Rose asked.

"Bitch on the patio spittin' mad G. She got it. Dripping head to toe in Purple – "

"I think I saw her. She wearing purple Lou's?" Summer asked.

"Yup. I'm a holler at her before we go," GG said.

"Bet. Hell, that's a couple of THOT G's, and a TLB. Shit, we gonna have plenty of new recruits up here before the night's over," Rose said. All the girls nodded in agreement and dug into the plate of BBQ. They walked through the house checking out the scene. Something different was going on in each room. There was an intense dice game on the kitchen floor, a hot orgy in the living-room (while Eddie Murphy's "Dolemite Is My Name" played on a 100-inch projection screen), drunk hopscotch in the foyer and people dancing in every corner of the place.

There were Cheetah and Zebra painted women crawling on the ceiling. Their magnetic kneepads kept them attached to the mirrored-glass ceiling as they erotically crawled on their hands and knees, circling each other. Some pawed each other or playfully kissed. It was hard for people ***not*** to look up and stare at the beautiful "jungle ass" jiggling above them. Shit was going down everywhere. But when the BBC walked into in the gameroom, what they witnessed made them smile.

"Hey, ma. You a bad bitch. And you did get the best of me with the Pizza Fight. Girl you hit hard as a motherfucka," Sharice said to Joy and massaged her cheek. They both laughed.

"Girl, you ain't no punk either. Shiiiid, you got me wit some good ones too," Joy said. The two women were conversing over drinks. Real recognized real, and in every challenge, someone has to win, and someone has to lose. It is the loser who determines whether they were a real challenger to begin with or not. Can you give the winner props for getting the best of you? Can you congratulate the champ holding the same trophy that you competed for? Or are you gonna hate and throw shade just because you didn't have what it took to get the W? A real motherfucker is going to congratulate (and not hate) their opponent. If you lose, step your game up and come back harder. If you get another opportunity, change the results in your favor.

LeBron didn't give up when the Spurs swept his ass the first time he went to the Finals. He kept striving, improved his game, and even got some "get back" against the same team that whooped his ass six years prior. But he didn't win them all. And that's what Sharice was able to express through her humble compliment.

"You know what? I can fuck with you girl. Do you want to exchange info?" Joy asked.

"Yeah," Sharice replied. They exchanged SnapChat's and made a toast to "new beginnings."

"See, now that's how you do it. If you take an L, don't go getting all salty cuz you lost and shit. Be like, 'you know what? You did your thang. You beat me fair and square. I ain't the biggest, baddest muthafucka in the world,' and keep it moving. Cuz even the biggest, baddest, muthafucka in the world can get beat on their worst day," Summer said.

"Preach mama!" GG said.

"Amen chica!" Rose shouted, raising her bottle in the air. To see two rivals get cool after going at each other's throats was a thing they didn't see too often. It made the Bad Bitchez Click feel good inside. There were more women like ***them*** after all. And in small ass towns at that.

"Look, we can both fuck Chauncey tonight. 'Ol pretty ass nigga. Let's see if he can handle *two* bad bitches at the same time," Joy said and laughed.

"Nah, ma. You won fair and square. Put it on him good for me," Sharice commented.

"You sure? Cuz I ain't like that. We can both buss that nigga down."

"Yeah, I'm sure. Good looking though," Sharice said.

"Aight then. Let me go find this nigga and put this pussy on his fine ass," Joy said.

"Go get him girl! Ride that dick goooood. You earned it," Sharice told Joy before exiting.

Rose, GG, and Summer nodded their approval at what they witnessed. Not wanting to crowd the gamers, they went to enjoy the rest of the after set and holler at Dab Daddy.

6

Feds Watching

I'm a be fresh as hell if the Feds watching...

"Who the fuck is the woman inside of your house talking to Carol Ma Baby?" Agent Christine Holis demanded. There was an iPad handed to Ma Baby who was in the back of an all-black Suburban truck. Special agent Bradshaw and his partner had come across some footage of Carol and was showing it to Ma Baby.

After she handed Becky over to the police, the Power Squad determined it was a "bogus fish" Ma Baby was trying to fry. A diversion of whoever was really doing all the dirt. So they began digging into surveillance tapes of old that they never reviewed. Besides the various men that were brought through for drugged-out threesomes, they discovered a gem. The first encounter of GG and Carol meeting at Walmart brought GG to Ma Baby's crib briefly.

Ma Baby held the 12.9-inch iPad Pro in her hands and watched as GG looked around her crib while Carol talked about nothing. Ma Baby knew it was old footage because of the décor, but she was totally curious as to what GG was doing in her house. And more importantly, why Carol failed to mention she had invited her in.

"I don't know that bitch. I guess my hoe was creeping around on me," Ma Baby said.

"Hmpf. How does that make you feel?" Agent Holis said with a smirk.

"Christine. For God's sake! Ma Baby, are you sure you don't know this woman?" Bradshaw asked, pausing the video to point at the screen. GG's curvaceous body was in a green Nike bodysuit. The wheels began turning in Ma Baby's head as she thought of various scenarios. Though none of them were accurate, she wanted to get to the bottom of GG's visit on her own time.

"Nah, never seen her before. Sorry."

"Well, *Carol* knew her obviously. We don't care what her snatch tastes like or how she licked on Carol's – "

"Bradshaw, if you don't get this bitch!" Ma Baby said, cutting off agent Holis.

"Ok, ok. Christine. Go for a walk, will ya?"

"What? I will not Bradshaw. I – "

"Goddamnit, let me handle this shit, Christine! Get your head out of your ass. You don't like her. She doesn't like you. But we need her, and you're pushing her away. Now go for a walk. Please, just take a hike," Bradshaw told his stubborn partner. Agent Holis sighed heavily and got out of the vehicle. She slammed the door and stomped off mumbling obscenities under her breath.

"I'm sorry about that. But look, we're just looking for some answers ok? The team is quite upset with you over the Slinkowski bust."

"I don't know why. The bitch is big up there. She – "

"Is the heir to a multi-unit Tanning Salon chain. Their family's money is legit. We've done all the digging we can do on them. The girl's like to smoke weed, but they're not drug dealers."

"Why, cuz they're young pretty white bitches? Is that why they can't be dealers? Psssh, whatever muthafucka. Y'all blind muthafuckas are something else. Anyways – "

"Anyways is right Rivera. Look, just see if you can find out who this is that Carol let into your house. She could be tied into her murder," Bradshaw said. Ma Baby shivered. A vivid flashback of Carol hanging in the air sent chills through her body. Ma Baby shook the image from her mind.

"I'll ask around," Ma Baby said.

Pig Shit had a meeting earlier in the day after one of the Tech guys discovered the video and brought it to Bradshaw. He played it for his team, and they were all told to find out who the woman in the video was. Bradshaw went straight to Ma Baby with it but got no results. What he didn't know, there actually *were* some members of the Power Squad who knew the woman in the video. Two men to be exact. But they weren't gonna tell Bradshaw, or anyone else that they knew who she was. Not yet at least.

~

THE CHAMPAGNE ROOM in Silk Exotic was a luxurious space of blue lights and glittery walls. Mirrors were on the ceiling and every wall. Leather swivel chairs sat side by side in front of small tables adorned with scented candles inside of glass votives.

Gushy was giving an erotic lapdance to the song "*M.P.A.*"

The handsome black man she was grinding against was a familiar face she'd been seeing a lot of lately. He and his big-eared friend were becoming her "regulars." Dropping serious cash every time they saw her.

"I love coming to see you. A beautiful black woman that looks and moves like you is a thing of beauty," he told her.

"Aww, thanks Daddy," Gushy said, putting her hand to his cheek and kissing him on his forehead.

"Now that I know you're more than just a stripper, I really look forward to seeing you," he said, grabbing her hips and grinding his erection into her leg.

"Um, what are you talking about baby?" Gushy asked him. She turned around and leaned her back into his chest while she held the arms of the chair. Her hips moved like she was hula hooping. She pressed her soft ass into his crotch. She could feel his slab of meat throb against her through his slacks.

"Well, I know you like to hang out at Ma Baby and Carol's crib. R.I.P. to that poor girl. You remember young Carol right?" The man she was dancing for shook his head and smiled devilishly. Gushy stood up quickly, but the black man grabbed her wrists and pulled her back into his lap. "Don't move too fast baby girl. My partner gets antsy when people jump up like that." The man's friend with the big ears was two chairs over getting a dance from a skinny blonde with big fake breasts. He tossed the woman on the floor and stood over Gushy in the blink of an eye. He threw some money at the white stripper and told her to get lost after flashing a badge. She grabbed her dough and got the hell up out of there.

"Who the fuck is y'all?" Gushy asked between gritted teeth.

"FBI. What the fuck it *look* like?" He said, flashing the gold shield inside of the black leather wallet.

"Shit!" Gushy exclaimed.

"Shit, is right, baby. But look, we ain't here to bust you. We just wanna talk. Hear us out and we all might be able to win."

"ARE YOU FUCKING SERIOUS CHICA? A real live oinker?" Rose asked.

"Yup, Pig Shit in the flesh. I'm telling you, that bitch Becky done –"

"Becky ain't said shit. You said they got you on tape inside Ma Baby's house right? Was that the only video they had of you?" Rose asked GG.

"Yeah..."

"And ain't no way they would've exposed their hand like that if they weren't really bout what they came to you with," Summer commented.

Tyrone Simmons was no longer just a regular client of Gushy's. As a member of Pig Shit, he and his cousin Sedrick were in the meeting when the tape of Carol and GG was shown. Even though the two were crooked Feds, that didn't mean they didn't still like to admire beautiful, thick women. They knew Gushy as soon as they saw her ass in that legging bodysuit. Tyrone elbowed his cousin who sat up straight and paid attention for the first time since Bradshaw spoke.

No one in the Power Squad knew of Tyrone and Sedrick's secret obsession for exotic dancers. The two cousins spent many of nights moonlighting in Stripclubs, blowing dirty money and getting their fix of naked women on the pole. Every black man in the country that had an appreciation for strippers knew who Gushy was. So, the discovery of Gushy and Carol on tape was like winning the lottery for Tyrone and Sedrick, a lottery that was to be kept a secret between the three of them.

When they escorted her out of Silk, she thought for sure that she was going to jail. But they had other plans for her.

"Yeah, we're the FBI. But we're not just any ol' Feds. Nah honey. We the muthafuckas you want on your team." Tyrone told Gushy. They were driving around in a 2020 Challenger

SRT Hellcat. Gushy was in the passenger seat, and Sedrick was in the back with his Bureau-issued Glock 17 on his lap. "We're an elite team that do shit *our* way. We need to bend the rules? They get bent. Somebody gotta get roughed up?" Tyrone shrugged.

"Wait, what do y'all call yourselves?" Gushy asked.

"The Power Squad," Tyrone and Sedrick responded simultaneously.

"Y'all Pig Shit?"

"Hey, hey. We don't like that name," Sedrick said defensively.

"Yeah, yeah, muthafucka. That's what y'all is ain't cha? Some dirty pigs? Don't sugar coat it. Come out wit it and say what you want," Gushy said, feeling bold now that she knew the type of individuals she was dealing with.

"No need to be disrespectful. We not calling you bitches and hoes."

"Go ahead. I am a bitch. And for the right price, I'll be the baddest hoe in the world!"

Agent Tyrone Simmons looked in the rear-view mirror at his partner Sedrick for assistance.

"Gushy, if you were one of the women involved in the Stripclub Capers we don't care. Give us some of the take, and we'll divert the attention away from you. While them dumb motherfuckers scramble around trying to find out who you are, we can help you stay two steps ahead. Otherwise, they're gonna find out who you are and..." Sedrick trailed off.

"Yeah, right. If *y'all* know who I am, your whole team does too," Gushy said.

"Uh-uh ma. That's where you're wrong. There are only a handful of minorities in P.S. and him and I are the only two *non*-Uncle Tom's." Tyrone said.

"Yeah, them other niggas so flaky. They agree with all the racist shit that's said and goes on in that bitch. We only tolerate it cuz we're in a position that can take us to another level. But those other motherfuckers are just dick-riding ass kissers," Sedrick told her.

"But that's your team though," Gushy said.

"Unfortunately. But it's most definitely a segregated team. We know we're needed for our skin color to get to certain people or get into certain places the white faces won't be welcomed in. Hey, at least we're not lying to ourselves saying it's because of our brains," Tyrone said and laughed. "It is what it is. We're just playing our positions until we get what we got into this for."

"And what's that?" Gushy asked.

Sedrick leaned over the seat. "Money, what else is there?" he said in her ear.

GG replayed the details of her meeting with Pig Shit to Rose and Summer.

"And you ain't give them no pussy?" Summer asked. The three of them were at The Green House for an emergency meeting. Rose was in Texas when GG called her about her ordeal. She chartered a jet straight back to the Mil. Summer was in Hawaii with Angelo, and they flew into Mitchell International ASAP.

"Naw girl. I was trying to, but them niggas wasn't going," GG responded.

"That worries me that they would pass up the opportunity to be with you," Rose said.

"Yeah, I was thinking that at first too. Then I thought about their whole demeanor and the passion in their plans...even though they like to *look* at pussy, I think these are a different breed of men. They have self-discipline. I was dancing to '*Money, Pussy, Alcohol*' when they stepped to me –"

"Wait, that Pusha T joint?" Summer asked.

"Yeah," GG replied.

"Ma, that ain't no dancing song," Rose said.

"Shiiiid, fuck what you talking about. It's slow and sexy, and that second verse when he spit for da bitches getting it how they live turns me *ON!*"

"I cancel all of you G money's for gee money," Rose rhymed.

"I get it done for quarter key money!" All three shouted in unison, quoting the song.

"Anyways, it's kinda ironic how all of that went down. I mean, they ***want*** to fuck, just not now. 'Ol boy was all like 'there will be a time and a place where we can have some fun', but they want to see if they could trust me or not first."

"Psssh, they must don't know who you is," Summer snorted.

"Obviously. I see the lust in their eyes when they talk though, but they really are on their business," GG said.

After making sure she wasn't tailed, GG went to her secret condo downtown after Pig Shit sent her on her way. At first, she was shook as fuck. She was looking out of her blinds every couple of minutes and checking every corner of the house for bugs and taps. She sent an encrypted text to her girls with the hashtag **#Fedz Watching.**

Once they all agreed to meet, GG went on a cleaning frenzy, making sure nothing dirty or incriminating was in her possession. While she wrestled with her thoughts on how them people got on to her, she kept coming back to their latest blue-eyed addition as the reason.

There was never any heat to the Bad Bitchez Click before Becky joined the family. Once she did, Ma Baby was free and in the picture, Summer had gotten shot, and now the Feds were on her ass. GG liked Becky, but she didn't think she should've come into the fold so quickly. But it was already done, and now she had to weigh her options because she worked too hard to go to prison or end up in a grave.

"They're the Money Over Bitches type. And with the disrespect from their colleagues fueling their fire, these brothers are carving out their own lane. I like it. This is the kind of opportunity we've been waiting to fall into our lap," Rose commented.

"Bitch, that's easy for you to say. You ain't the ones they watching!" GG said irritated.

"Mami, calm your ass down. Don't nobody but them two clowns know who you are, and even they don't really know shit. Now we're gonna get all the dirt we can on them and use it to our advantage. You're gonna have to go the extra mile to wear their defenses down and put that Gushy on them though," Rose informed her.

"I already know. We gonna have to go Operation Paparazzi with them," GG said.

"Nah, we could just do some secret recording for them. They're the ones trying to do the extorting," Summer said.

"True. We'll figure out how to proceed with them once we find out what we need to know about them," Rose said.

"Mhm. Girl, I'm stressing for real for real. Y'all got some of them dab cubes? A bitch need to get higher than research monkeys right now!" GG said, pulling out a bag of BBC bomb and some Honey Berry Backwoods.

"I gotchu," Summer said, digging into her Michael Kors bag. She sat a denture case on the table. It was full of Dab Daddy's caramel-looking creations. "Relax boo. We gonna get to the bottom of this shit. They already got one of us in the belly of the beast. We won't let them snatch another."

"Damn skippy peanut butter! They gonna have to kill me if they think I'm going," GG announced, loading an extended clip into her 9mm.

"Hell yeah girl," Rose agreed, cocking her own Desert Eagle. "Shit about to get real funky round this bitch!"

7

18 With A Bang!

THIS WAS by far the biggest bash the Bad Bitchez Click had ever thrown, and for a great cause, it was Brix' 18th Birthday. You only become "legal" once in a lifetime. For the women who started out as "girls" and blossomed into GROWN ASS WOMEN, to be 18 was a grand celebration that they planned to honor to the max!

Under "Boss Chicks Realty" the BBC built a state-of-the-art Nightclub in Appleton that rivaled the ones in Miami and California. "Club Drip" was an exclusive Nightclub for the party people who left their inhibitions at the door. With diverse levels of culture, each floor brought a Drip in only the way it's true attendees could *feel*. A four-story palace that housed four different Nightclubs catered to various crowds. When you entered Club Drip, there was an automatic $10 entry fee. This allowed you to access the four clubs unless you wanted V.I.P.

(BeeHive). That was in a different building where the ballers and ambitious hustlers lounged at.

Once you paid your ten, a beautiful employee gave you a purple wristband. You then entered the first floor where "Zig-Zahm" was housed. Zig-Zahm was an all-purpose kind of bar. There were four pool tables, four dart boards, a small dance-floor, and Karaoke (whenever someone requested a song). Zig-Zahm also had a mini-restaurant, and that's the only place in the building you could get food at.

A concrete stairwell took you to whatever level you wanted to go to. On the second floor was "The Barnyard." A big ass country bar with a barn theme. The barstools were fake hay and a mechanical bull sat in the middle of the dancefloor. In the back was a Horse & Carriage that walked a vacant corridor that led to the balcony. The Horse & Carriage was $100 for a 20-minute ride. But it was a great "extra" for the guys who wanted to do something special and different for their lady. A romantic gesture that was very popular and a main reason girls would drag their boyfriend's to "The Barnyard," (to say they got on the Horse & Carriage).

On the third floor was "Litty Block." That was for the younger turn-up crowd. Mostly people under 25 got lit to Trippie Redd and Da Baby tracks. There was a big stage where artists performed at, whenever they came to do a poppin' ass show in Appleton.

The fourth floor was "The Ballers House." An elegant players lounge with velvet couches, big screen Televisions all over the walls, 20-foot ceilings with contemporary art painted on it, and sexy, half-naked servers (with lace Venetian Masquerade masks), catered to a more luxurious clientele than the other floors. The Baller's House is where the D boys and money getting people hung out at — popping bottles, jamming to music, smoking Hookahs, and making moves. The whole club was a savvy business move and work of art, put together by none other than a team of Bad Boss Chicks.

They bought the old College football facility that closed down years prior. Three acres of land was turned into a party playground of epic proportions! The training facility was turned into the V.I.P. building (tentatively named "BeeHive"), where guests were shuttled to via limos and golf carts (once they paid the $100 admission fee at Club Drip). V.I.P.'s were given bracelets that allowed them into the lavish club halfway across the property.

BeeHive was built by money *having* muthafuckas, for money *getting* muthafuckas. The front lobby contained a 30-foot waterfall, where huge Koi fish swam in a fountain beneath it. The interior was a futuristic design done by their homegirl Kim, an Architect and interior design student they put through school.

Huge chandeliers covered in Swarovski crystals *and* LED lights (that flashed to the beat of music playing) blinged from the ceiling. Bikini-clad dancers with gothic make-up and Go-go boots danced inside of gold cages. A Skybox (where the DJ rocked the house) overlooked an elaborate dancefloor that was always full. Twenty cabanas surrounded a glittering swimming pool in the middle of the club. There was a private locker room for the guests to use and change into their swim attire, and a small gift shop that sold swimsuits, blunts, cigarettes and other knick-knacks as well.

The best thing people liked about Beehive was there were no glasses. Guests got served full bottles and had to drink out of those. There were no cups, no shot glasses... just bottles ONLY! And that was fine by the upper echelon of attendees who came to enjoy the fruits of their labor with other like-minded individuals. Broke people couldn't afford to spend $110 to get into a Nightclub. So those that did go to BeeHive knew they were in good company, and the atmosphere was always "Ballerific" and peaceful.

"SCARY ASS NIGGA, ain't you trying to go harder than Young Thug and nem did in they '*Hot*' video?" Summer questioned Matt.

"Yeah fam. You know Thugger had the Slime Fire truck and walked through the spot on fire," Bucky replied, slipping on his custom jacket for the show.

"I know, but that was a fireman suit. These..."

"Pussy, these are the real deal Holyfield's muthafucka," GG said, getting frustrated. She slipped on the suede jacket and zipped it up. "Not only are these fireproof, but it'll take some hot ones too. Here," GG pulled a .45 out and cocked it. "Shoot me," she extended the gun to Matt.

"Huh? Wh-what? No, Gushy I – "

"Damn Bucky, your crew soft as a bitch my nigga. All that hot air about being down and shit, but these niggas wouldn't squeeze a fat *ass*, let alone a *trigger*," GG said and laughed. Summer and Rose joined in for added effect. They were backstage at "Litty Block" and the BBC were prepping Pill Mobb for their first ever live performance.

GG had talked Bucky into dipping his toe into the rap game. With the help of Party HaRRRd and Hollywood Peru, they wrote and produced a banging ass EP for the click of white boys who loved rap but didn't know how to *make* it. GG, Summer, and Rose worked with them in terms of moves, swag, and style, until they could pass for half-way decent rappers. It was a lot of work, but it was all for a bigger, more profitable plan.

Pill Mobb had already recorded three unreleased music videos, two of which would debut at Brix' party. But GG told Bucky and them they should shoot a live video for their "Pill

Mobb On Fiya" song. Summer had supplied them with Miguel Caballero outfits made of Columbian Kevlar. Colorful Suede jackets with PM and their individual names on them went with matching suede and velvet joggers.

When they rehearsed for the fire performance days earlier, it was in actual fireman suits, but once it was time to put on what they'd actually be wearing, one of the members got cold feet.

"Bro, you're making us look bad in front of our ladies man," Lincoln said. Rose was zipping up his jacket for him and whispering in his ear about Matt.

"Nigga, shoot me. That way your square ass will know this jacket can take on anything," GG threatened Matt. She stood over him with a cocked pistol in her hand.

"Um, no Gushy. It's alright. I'll – "

"Man, my bitch said pop her. So, go ahead and pop the hoe," Bucky said, snatching the gun out of GG's hand. ***Pop! Pop! Pop!*** He put three bullets into GG. One in the arm and two in the chest. She fell to one knee, hunched over and holding her chest.

"F-Fuck Bucky. You..." GG wheezed.

Bucky dropped the gun on the floor and rushed to Gushy's side. "Shit! Baby, are you ok? I didn't mean to – "

"Ha haaaa, I got your ass fool," she said, sticking her tongue out and hitting him on the arm playfully.

"Woman, that shit ain't funny. You scared the crap out of me girl," Bucky said.

"Awww, daddy. Nice of you to be so concerned after you done shot a bitch."

"Well, you da one egging niggas on and shit. You know I'm a pop dat thang!"

"I see that, daddy. See, y'all *leader* bout that life," Gushy said, walking up to all the Pill Mobb members so they could touch the bullet-riddled jacket.

"Ya see, no need to worry Matt. When y'all do Pill Mobb on fiya, you going viral with this one. Rocking the mic with flames on your Tommy Hilfiger suits gonna turn y'all into overnight sensations," Rose said.

"Yeah, you're right. My bad for acting like a bitch you guys," Matt told them and stood up. GG took off the jacket she just got shot in and put it on Matt. She zipped it up and gave him a light peck on the lips.

"Hey, hey now," Bucky whined.

"Aww, nigga be quiet. You a player ain't you? Don't go acting funny cuz yo bitch showing your guy some love," Summer said.

"Huh? I'm not trippin. It's all good. I don't give a fuck about that shit," Bucky said, trying to swallow the jealous lump in his throat that formed when Gushy kissed his friend.

"Mmhm, whatever nigga. Anyways, I hope y'all ready to do this shit. It's our girl's birthday. We picked tonight to debut y'all shit cuz it's a special night," Rose said.

"Yo, we ready ma. It's gonna be epic!" Bucky said, raising his Henny bottle in the air.

"Yo, where is Brix anyway? Does she not want her presents?" Lincoln inquired.

"She's spending some one on one time with her sister. But I'm finna go get her. Y'all get the cake ready and shit, GG said.

"THIS IS YOUR NIGHT BRIT-BRIT. You are finally legal," Becky laughed, stroking her sister's long hair. Brix was sitting at a Hollywood make-up vanity mirror, analyzing her newly done eggplant colored hairstyle. Kayla B had done her hair and had it on fleek! Becky stood behind her younger sister in a skintight, sky-blue, satin mini-dress and matching heels.

Becky was supposed to bail out three weeks ago but decided not to. She didn't think she'd live long enough to see her little sister turn eighteen. The stakes were high and too many people were on her ass. There was even a bounty put out on her head by the Milwaukee Mami's for fifty G's. She knew her time was limited and wanted to give her sister a special gift on her birthday. So, she chose to post bond the day before.

She walked out of Federal custody in pink Timberland heel boots and a matching jogging suit. Gail, Tom, and Becky's high-priced lawyer were all there to pick her up. She noticed immediately the white car that followed them all the way home. Brix was in Eau Claire at the time of Becky's release, but she made it back in the middle of the night for a heartfelt discussion. Some stuff she held back for the birthday bash.

"Yup, even though I've been on my grown woman stuff, thanks to you and GG nem, I am now *official,*" she said and laughed.

"You sure are. Tonight is a big night for you. I hope you're prepared..." Becky trailed off as emotions welled up inside her and tears slid down her cheeks. Brix looked in the mirror at her only sibling. She could only imagine the hurt and pain she felt.

"Fuck all them niggas we gon' fuck up this cash, I hopped out my feelings and I hopped in my bag. Hopped in a foreign bitch you hopped in a cab, still living with your mama you ain't hopped off your ass. Aye!"

Cuban Doll could be heard performing while Brix and Becky chopped it up in the back office of Litty Block. A sharp knock on the door made them both jump.

"Can I come in bitches?" GG said, closing the door behind her. "Bucky crazy as a muthafucka. That nigga really did shoot me," GG said, rubbing her chest plate.

"What?" Becky and Brix said in shock.

"Don't worry y'all, I'm good. Matt was being a pussy about performing in them outfits, so I had to do a demonstration for his ass," GG told them and walked into the small office bathroom. Becky sighed and sat down at the oak desk. She looked at

Brix through the vanity mirror. They stared in each other's eyes, neither one blinked until GG came out of the bathroom.

"It's about that time," GG said. Becky nodded solemnly and pulled a Glock out of the drawer and put the barrel under her chin.

"GG, you have to know that I never said a word, and I never would. I swear to God –"

"Becky, I don't know *shit*. Ever since we welcomed you in, it's been one thing after another. Too much negative energy follows you. We can't have that shit."

"I understand," Becky nodded slowly. "Really, I do. This is what I signed up for. I just don't understand why we can't do this another way. We're smart. I know we can..."

"What Becky? Huh? It's too much heat on us now. We have to cool things off cuz we got shit to do. We're not letting anything or *anyone* stop us." GG walked up to Brix and stroked her hair. "I like this new color on you Mami."

"Thanks," Brix said, fidgeting with her hands in her lap. She couldn't look up, so she just stared at her purple and grey Air Force One's.

Becky stood up and held the Glock to her temple. "There is a video I left for you guys on there," she nodded towards the MacBook Pro on the desk. "For what it's worth, I don't regret taking an oath to the Bad Bitches Click," Becky moved the gun down the front of her dress and revealed the BBC tattoo on her left breast.

"Everything happens for a reason. You came into the fold so we could take this to the next level. Too bad you won't be around to see it. Really sorry it had to come to this, but we can't take penitentiary chances on you. Now do it!" GG demanded as she reached into her purse.

Becky put the gun back to the side of her own head. "I love you, Britney." ***Click!*** Becky pulled the trigger and flinched, fully expecting her brains to splatter all over the office walls. She opened her eyes and stared at GG and Brix. She pulled the trigger again. And again. ***Click...click.*** Becky looked down the barrel of the gun in bewilderment.

"How did I know you would chicken out," GG sighed and pulled a revolver from her purse. Brix stood up and put a hand on top of GG's gun.

"I've got this," Brix said, pulling her own gun out and pointing it at Becky. "I couldn't let you off yourself Becks, so I took the bullets out." Brix walked toward her sister. "I don't know what the afterlife has in store for you, but I'd hate for you to go to hell because you had to pull your own trigger." ***Rarr! Rarr!*** Brix fired off two shots, hitting Becky in the chest, sending her flying into the wall.

"I'm so sorry sis. But you were right about a couple of things, it is ride or die for you." ***Rarr!*** "And I *will* be a badder bitch than you." ***Rarr!*** Brix put another bullet between Becky's eyes as she stood over her lifeless body and shed silent tears. GG stood next to Brix and aimed her revolver at the deceased Becky. ***Rarr! Rarr!***

"Had to make sure it was official," GG commented.

"Um, do you not see that bloody hole in her forehead?" Brix asked.

"Yeah, but that shit could be fixed. In movies, they have fake bullets that explode red dye upon contact." Brix rolled her eyes at GG. "Whaaaat? A lot of muthafuckas do that shit when they fake their own death. Anyway, damn. I didn't see *that* coming. You alright?"

"As well as I can be after murdering my own sister."

"Damn. Your day one. Shit, you crazy as hell girl. Ya, see. Them fuck niggas done rubbed off on you. Mmmhm, I know they did. Why didn't you just let her do it?"

"I couldn't GG. We don't believe you can go to heaven if you off yourself. Besides, I wanted y'all to know how down I was for this shit. You wanted her gone? Well, *I* took her out. So, I deserve her spot," Brix said. As much as she hated to admit it, Becky's "Jealous Ones Envy" speech was a real ass declaration that resonated deep in her soul. Brix knew she would forever be in her big sister's shadow. She wanted to branch out and be her *own* woman. As long as Becky was around, Brix would forever be the Solange to her sister's "Beyoncé.

The weeks spent studying under GG brought more than walking in heels lessons. Brix knew her sister was going to die. With the bounty on her head and BBC being leery about her, it was inevitable that she would be murdered upon her release. So, Brix whipped up a plan to get rid of Becky herself. She was surprised that she actually went through with it though.

"Hmpf. Well, we have business to attend to, so let's clean this up and go open your gifts," GG said. "Everyone's waiting for you."

"Yay! Presents always cheer a bitch up. And I kinda need it right now," Brix replied.

"...*Happy birthday dear Bri-i-x. Happy birthday to you*," the whole room sang.

"Awww, thank you guys. Even your off-key singing ass Bucky."

"Ha, ha. You're soooo funny. Anyways, happy birthday Brix. I hope you like it," Bucky said, handing her a big, pink wrapped box. Inside was $1,800 from each Pill Mobb member and 18 prescription bottles all filled to the brim with various pills.

"Heyyy now. Thanks y'all," Brix told them.

"Ok, ok. Open mine next," Summer said, handing Brix a glittery gift bag.

She opened the card first and smiled big at the vulgar Spencer's Birthday card. "What's this?" Brix inquired about the gift card inside.

"Well, I know how much you love your sneakers girl. And since you in Eau Claire a lot, you can hit up my guy's store."

"Drip Kickz?"

"Mhm. They be having all the exclusive color J's, Air Max, and Air Force Ones."

"Oh ok. How much is on here," Brix asked, looking at the gift card.

"It's unlimited. You can buy as many shoes as you want. Whenever you want."

"Dang, really? What if I want everything in the store?" Brix said and laughed.

"Shiiid, buy the store then ma," Summer shrugged. "They just gonna have to close til they get more inventory. Now come on, show everyone what else is in the bag."

"Ok." Brix pulled out a rectangular box and ripped the wrapping paper off.

"Since you ain't really got no dude, I figured that would come in handy," Summer smiled.

"Holy shit! You put it out already?"

"Nah, not yet. You're receiving the first one," Summer said, referring to her "Duck-Me" sex toy invention. "I'll be throwing a release party for it in about a month when it's ready for mass distribution. You better have your ass there."

"Of course. On my sister's life I wouldn't miss it for nothing in the world," Brix said and winked at GG. "Summer, you know I'm gonna be up in that bitch."

"That's what that toy in your hand is saying now," Summer said, making everyone laugh.

"Here you go mami. Happy Birthday." Rose sat a box on Brix' lap.

"Thanks Summer. I can't wait to try it out. Maybe I'll rub one out in the new kicks I get from that store." Brix commented and opened Rose's gift. Everyone's eyes got big. "Um..."

"Well, I know you said you would handle that nigga Gates

for selling fake dope to your peeps, but I found out he did some bogus shit to my bish in THOT Gang. That's a souvenir."

Brix held up a gold Cuban link necklace that had a pair of hairy testicles dangling from it like it was a medallion. "Damn, Rose. You cut the niggas nuts off?"

"Well, not personally. I had 'ol girl Trudy do it while she sucked his dick." (Trudy was a 4'3" dwarf in the Little Onez clique.) "When I confronted the mog, he got all slick at the mouth. Telling me, he was A-1 and all he had was his balls and his words and all that bullshit. Well, his word is *basura*. And now, he ain't got no balls, so..." Rose shrugged nonchalantly.

The room grew uncomfortably silent while Brix put the necklace on. "You could have shaved these hairy motherfuckers," Brix said, scratching her chest.

"Wanted them in their original form," Rose commented. "Check out your new bag mami."

Brix took the necklace off and put it back into its specially made glass case. A tan Crocodile skin Louis Vuitton handbag was also inside the box. Brix felt the material and moaned. When she opened it, her eyes damn near popped out of her head.

"That's 1.8 million Mami," Rose whispered in Brix' ear, referring to the cash stuffed inside.

"Thank you so much, Rose." Brix stood up and hugged the sexy Latina.

GG was standing next to the table her gift was on. "Last but not least. Come on over here and see what Auntie GG got for you."

"Oooh, what is it?" Brix said, taking the wrapping paper off.

"I know how you said you always wanted to deep fry a turkey."

"Oh... yeah. Ok." The disappointment on Brix' face was evident as she looked at the 30-quart Turkey fryer.

"Girl, open it up," GG said. Brix did as she was told, and

everyone crowded around her as she took the lid off. GG pulled a big glass container out of the turkey fryer and sat it on the table. Brix dropped the lid on the floor, and everyone in the room took a step back. The glass jar was full of liquid, and contained the decapitated head of her ex-boyfriend Gutter. His gold and diamond teeth glistened in the murky fluid his head floated in.

"I know you gave the nigga a pass by letting him join the Fuck Nigga Boyz, but his dis-loyalty towards you is something I just couldn't honor Brix. Every time I saw this clown flexing on Instagram and Snapchat, it just made my blood boil! Nah, fuck-boy. You can't do what you did to one of mines and get away with it."

"We don't spare no nigga. Cut his head off and show me it's real," Bucky rapped. "Whaaat? She's the one cutting niggas heads off and shit. I just –"

"Whatever Bucky," Brix cut him off. "Fuckin ay GG, what am I supposed to do with it?" Brix questioned her mentor.

"Shiiid, either keep it as is, or if I was you, I'd deep fry that muthafucka and send it to his mama for Thanksgiving!" Everyone in the room was creeped out yet interested at the same time. "Oh, and here girl. I hope you didn't think a bitch was just gon' get you a Turkey fryer." GG handed Brix a small box that contained the key fob to a Lamborghini truck.

"You gotta be shitting me! Is this?..."

"Mhm. I know how you been wanting the Lamb truck, but they've been on backorder. Got yours moved to the front of the line."

"Awww, thanks GG. You're the best." Brix said, hugging GG.

"You're welcome girl. You know you my 'lil white mini-me. Now go cut your cake and put me up a fat ass piece."

"Everything taken care of?" Rose whispered to GG when Brix walked off.

"Yup," GG nodded and stared at her protégé from across the room.

"She really did it, or you had to?"

"Naw, she did it. Thought she was gon' chicken out, but she Kurt Cobaine'd her brain for real for real," GG told Rose. "But let me ask you something. What made you change your mind about wanting her gone? I *been* saying the shit, but y'all was like naw she cool, fall back."

"Because there can only be one, and it's always been Brix," Rose admitted. "Well, originally it was supposed to be Becky, but the day I met Becky, I also met her sister. I saw the heart and courage of that girl when she got her ass kicked. I knew she was ***thee*** one. She hadn't been through shit yet, and she was younger too, so we could mold her. Brix had the look of Becky that we needed, but she was also green because of her youth. I knew once we took her under our wing, she would surpass Becky. Her ambition and heart has always been on full display. Even though this Ma Baby shit put a monkey wrench in the game, it's perfect timing. Someone was gonna have to go eventually." Rose shrugged.

Heart and ambition is an understatement, GG thought to herself. She didn't tell Rose that it wasn't a suicide, but rather a cold-blooded Bee sting (that also happened to be murder) that took Becky out. She was no rat; that minor variation would be her and Brix' dirty little secret.

~

I'm in the Caddy with Addie (Ay!)
The Mobb Pop an Addy with Addie (Ay!)
She calling me Daddy 'Her Pappy?'(Nay!)
PM got them Addy's hey Addie 'Heyyy'

. . .

Pill Mobb was on stage performing their hit song "Addie." The music video for their song played on the giant screen above the stage. It was the first time anyone had seen it. All the hard work spent becoming rappers had paid off. Choreographed dance lessons took hours a day. The studio became their first home, and thanks to Party HaRRRd's lyrics and Hollywood Peru's beats, the Pill Mobb's debut album was slamming!

They rapped about what they did, so it was authentic words that people felt. All the kids in Appleton who popped pills, loved to party, and "turn up," were loving that Pill Mobb shit. It came from people they could relate to. Their *peers*. It spoke to a culture that was living what Pill Mobb rapped about, and they couldn't get enough!

GG thought it would be a goldmine to turn some hip-hop loving white dudes from the middle of nowhere, into a corporate money earning rap group. And as the first act under their Mobb $hit Records, Pill Mobb had made Lipstick Enterprises a mint! They were doing 50,000 units a week, and that didn't count the half mill they did their first week out. Not bad for some pill-popping puppets. Rose and Summer were quite pleased with GG's candid idea. Music money was a great addition to their empire.

GG and Summer were on stage when Pill Mobb performed their songs. They were the girlfriends of the main rappers, so they had to represent and make the boys look good. Having a hot video vixen and a renowned stripper as their main pieces gave Pill Mobb more street cred and lots of fans. GG had turned Bucky's "Drip" up to astronomical proportions. So it was no surprise when he drove girls nuts like he was Channing Tatum or something. Ahh, the illusions that fame made.

"Give it up for my dudes, the hottest rap group out here. Pill Mobb!" GG shouted to the crowd. Bucky and his boys followed suit and yelled "Pill Mobb!"

Summer spoke to the crowd next. "We about to shoot the

last music video y'all. For those of you who didn't sign a waiver, you need to do so now or leave, cuz whoever in this bitch for 'Pill Mobb On Fiya' gonna be videotaped."

A few people made their way to the exit, but the majority stayed and got closer to the stage. Pretty girls distributed complimentary Champagne bottles with sparklers in them to the crowd. The lights dimmed, and a white spotlight shone toward the corner wall in back of the stage. A giant LED covered chair came out of the ceiling and dangled above the crowd. Brix was in it making it rain blunts and dab cubes to the people down below.

"Mami," Rose began, looking up at the floating chair. "Today, you are no longer a nina. This is the day you become a mujer. A jefa –"

"A grown ass woman!" GG shouted over Rose's shoulder.

"Sí. A grown ass woman for sure. But much more though. Tonight, we celebrate a new chapter in your life. New beginnings turn into old endings. But from this day forward, you paint your destiny. Happy Birthday ma. To Brix!" Rose raised her Champagne bottle and everyone in Litty Block did so as well.

"To Brix!" They all toasted to the birthday girl in grand fashion.

"Look, we want to thank everyone for making tonight a special night for our girl. All the performers, servers and people behind the scenes who put this shit together, much love y'all." Summer said into the mike. "We finna kick this shit off tho. If you ain't heard the song Pill Mobb On Fiya, then yo ass been on Mars!" The crowd began screaming as soon as she said the title of the song. "But we finna set this bitch on fire toniiiii-iiiight!"

The whole club went completely dark, and a hard, thunderous bass line rumbled from the speakers. ***Boom Booooooooom. Boom Boooooooooom.***

. . .

"I GOT FIRED cuz of pills, hey Pill Mobb you got me fired.
Someone please make it rain, cuz Pill Mobb is on fiya!"

BRIX' pre-recorded voice for the "Pill Mobb On Fiya" chorus rocked the club while the boys got into position. Summer, GG and Rose exited the stage and stood behind the Cameramen.

Bucky recruited his own group of white girls to be extras in the music video. They were on stage, high, drunk, excited, and turnt up. It was a great visual. The cameramen captured the performance on several cameras from multiple views.

The stage was lined with strobe lights and pyrotechnics. As soon as the first verse came in, the pyro display began to shoot off lightning bolts of sparkling, colorful excitement. The special custom-made jackets Pill Mobb wore ignited with small flames. The crowd went bonkers, watching them rock the mike while fire danced on their clothes.

IT'S BOSS BUCKY BITCH, I only fuck Boss chicks
I'll wet you up for my Ruffles, damn I hate soggy chips...

BUCKY HAD THE LAST VERSE, and when he was done, a big fireworks showcase was going to light up the stage. In the meantime, sparklers shot from Pill Mobb's arms and legs.

BITCH MY HAIR IS RED, is my head not fire?
I'm a Pill Mobb nigga, come let me get you higher.

. . .

Brix was bobbing her head as she watched the show from up above. She picked up a tiny remote control and pointed it at the stage. Everyone in Pill Mobb tensed up. The inside of each members jacket suctioned them in.

I...I'm hotter than a fire. Pill Mobb bitch, we...on...fiya

Bucky wheezed as he managed to squeeze his last bars out. He and the others were trying to unzip their jackets (that were literally sucking the life out of them), but they weren't coming off. The garments that Angelo told Summer about were great weapons that were tweaked by the BBC and tailor-made for Pill Mobb. With the click of a button, it could suck the oxygen from inside the garment, or ignite flames from tiny valves implanted in the fabric.

Brix had the remote that shut down the inside of their outfits. Rose had a remote that turned the gas up on their valves. Without warning, orange balls of fire shot from every Pill Mobb members clothes. Women screamed, and people began to run. When Pill Mobb attempted to "Stop, drop, and roll," the floor ignited in a blinding fury of light. ***Whoooooosh!***

The pyrotechnics shot colorful sparks into the ring of fire, outlining the stage. Lincoln stumbled into Matt and the two friends burst into flames. As Matt became a Cau-*Cajun*, he couldn't help but think back on the warning he gave his crew about the fire shoot. He watched his entire clique burn. The flammable acoustic foam along the walls helped spread the fire quickly and evenly.

Panic set in. A stampede for the exit took place as black smoke filled the club, and people trampled over one another. Rose looked up at the ceiling. Brix and the chair were no longer there. She pushed another button on her remote and all of the sparklers left in the bottles throughout the club lit up at once. Bottles exploded. Shards of glass flew in the air like confetti as hot fireballs bounced around like video game effects.

"Pill Mobb on fire! Pill Mobb on fire!" A frantic man screamed as he ran downstairs.

"Hell yeah, Pill Mobb on fiya. That's my song!" A blue-haired girl said, not knowing he was speaking in the *literal* sense.

Bucky's screams were silenced by the fire that seared his tongue off. He coughed and groaned while his skin melted like candlewax. He lay on his side, watching flames wave at him from all directions. The last thing he saw before he left earth was some blond hair covering him like a blanket. Then a pair of purple and grey Nike shoes ran toward the entrance.

Outside, firetrucks, ambulances, and squad cars pulled into the parking lot where hundreds of people milled about. Friends consoled one other while others prayed their peeps made it out of the club safely. Front and center was Brix. Rose was on her left side, and Summer was on her right. They massaged her back and shoulders, hoping to calm her.

"Anyone seen my sister? Where's my sister? Is Becky still in there? Somebody help my sister!" Brix shouted frantically. Her 18th Birthday sash clung to her curves, and her crown hung from her head crookedly. She pulled them both off and threw them behind her. "Fuck this shit. I'm coming Becky!" Brix shouted as she ran toward the entrance. Paramedics tried to block her, but she escaped their grasp and ran into the smoking building anyways. Rose and Summer looked at each other. It was time for them to get ghost.

8

Masterminds

THANKS, Jen. The heroics of an Appleton teenager at Club Drip last week has brought forth lots of community support. Her family, Tom and Gail Slinkowski, of Sunset Tanning Salon, are asking for cash donations to contribute to their daughter's trauma. Rebecca, the 29-year-old daughter, was burned alive at the Pill Mobb pyrotechnics show. Her funeral will be held this weekend.

Britney Slinkowski was celebrating her 18th Birthday day party at the club when a stage malfunction caused a huge fire to erupt during the performance. After escaping safety, Britney braved the flames again -despite authorities warning her- in efforts to save her sister who was still inside.

A surviving couple was rescued by Britney when she kicked down a bathroom door that was barricaded by a fallen beam. She told them to breathe into their shirts and run for help.

Britney lost conscience in her quest to find her sister. Firefighters were able to rescue Britney from the deadly blaze that claimed twenty-two lives. She sits in Intensive Care with third-degree burns on 90% of her body...

"DAMMMMN, Y'ALL SOME BAD MUTHAFUCKAS," Chula commented, after turning the TV down. She was sitting in a hospital bed surrounded by Rose, Summer and a disguise wearing Brix and GG. The whole club fiasco was nationwide news.

"Damn right we is. Do you know how much muthafuckin' money is coming in for the Slinkowski fund?" GG said.

"My sister had a genius idea with that one," Brix remarked. When Becky found out how many supporters were behind her while she was in jail, she blueprinted a plan to use her family's wealthy connections as a way to fund her clicks future.

"Yeah. 'Ol Becky. Damn. How you feeling ma?" Chula asked Brix.

"I'm alright," she shrugged. "Kinda numb to the shit by now ya know?"

"Yeah, I can only imagine what you're going through," Chula said to Brix, who was dressed like an emo-goth chick in her black wig, make-up, and clothes.

"Anyways, fuck all that. Girl, how are you and the baby doing?" Summer asked. Chula was three months pregnant. Some masked men kicked in her door and beat her to a pulp, almost killing her and the baby.

"The doctor said we'll be fine. There were some minor injuries, but nothing a tough bitch can't handle," Chula smiled through busted lips. One of her eyes was swollen shut, and she had three fractured ribs.

"That's good. We have people looking into the tattoo descriptions you told us about," Rose said. During the home invasion, Chula noticed tattoos on the robbers' forearms whenever their sleeves slid up. They demanded to know where the pounds of weed were. Not happy with the two bricks she handed over, they smacked her around until she led them to the *real* stash spot. They tied her up and got away with 30 pounds of top-shelf marijuana.

"You ain't seen yo baby daddy?" GG asked Chula.

"Nope. After our argument last week, I ain't even heard from the nigga."

"Kk. Well, we gon' see who did this and handle it for you," GG responded. "Whaaat?"

"Girl, no offense, but you look ridiculous," Chula commented.

"She's kinda right. You look like Lil Kim with a mop on," Summer said and laughed.

"Fuck y'all. I got them people on my ass. Shiiiid, I'm trying to float under the radar," GG said, running her fingers through her gray wig. Blue coke bottle glasses covered her eyes, and a baggy sweatsuit hid her dangerous curves.

"So, who's the girl in the hospital bed?" Chula asked Brix.

"An SBG fan. She don't got what it take for this street shit, but she wanna be down sooooo bad. That's why we used her body as a decoy," Brix said. Under a carefully master-minded plan, the Bad Bitchez Click killed two birds with one stone by eliminating Pill Mobb *and* Becky.

After accumulating the information needed to hit Pill Mobb's inventory, the rap factor was added as a gimmick to justify their deaths. The "fire-proof" suits were actually fatal garments that suffocated each member and burned them to a crisp. Pill Mobb's stash houses were hit the day after the club fire. Hundreds of thousands of dollars' worth of pills would soon hit the streets for the low-low, courtesy of Bucky and his crew. But most importantly, Appleton was in dire need of a pill supplier with the J-Twins, Becky, and Pill Mobb all deceased. Someone would take their spots and make a *killing*.

The burned-up girl thought to be Britney (covered head to toe in excruciating burns), was actually Claudia Zuner. A young white girl who pledged her love and loyalty to Snow Bunny Gangstaz. She had the perfect height and dimensions to pass for Britney, so they made Claudia sacrifice her body to pull off their con.

The remains of "Becky" was a junkie chick from Eau Claire. She was drugged, kidnapped, stripped of her teeth, shaved completely bald, and stuffed in a tote. After Becky's murder, GG and Brix swapped the junkie's body for Becky's. They made sure hair and teeth (that would be verified as Becky's) were left on the "dummy" body that Brix laid on top of Bucky. Becky's actual corpse was stored in a fire-proof safe that was lowered underground in a secret chute.

Over $100,000 of donations poured in to help pay for hospital bills and the funeral costs.That amount climbed by the day. The Slinkowski's already had burial packages for the whole family, and the girl fighting for her life at St. Elizabeth wouldn't be around much longer. So, all of that money would be used as investment capital for the next BBC venture.

Thanks to the demise of Patricia Clooney and the twins, the hospital was in need of employees immediately. A woman by the name of Lissa was picked to supersede Patty. Lissa was put through school by the BBC and had a few years' experience in the medical field. Strings were pulled, palms were greased, and dicks were sucked, to get Lissa in the running for the job. Now she was given an entire hospital to run. Her job was to hire women affiliated with the fam, amplify Patty's previous pill operation, and keep visitors away from "Britney's" room. The full-figured woman was so grateful for her current opportunity; she would've agreed to whatever the Bad Bitchez Click wanted.

The way they eliminated Pill Mobb was one for the record books. What started out as a plot to get rid of their competition, turned into a financial plan of longevity. Because they were a bunch of hip white kids, Pill Mobb became *more* famous through their deaths (as most musicians do than in their actual lives). Their music shot to the top of the charts and was in heavy rotation on all of the mainstream outlets. This brought in a substantial amount of income to Mob $hit Records. And because BBC owned the Pill Mobb name and all of their publishing rights, Bucky and nem would be paying those Boss chicks for years to come!

9

Ashes To Ashes

EMINEM'S *"DARKNESS"* played in the background as pictures and videos of Becky, aka Rebecca Marie Slinkowski, flashed on the projection screen in the church. Brix picked the unusual song to go with the slideshow of memories she put together.

Brix's behavior and movements as a severe burn victim could've won her an Academy Award. Escorted by her parents, Brix limped slowly to the podium. She held onto the walker tightly as she made her way up the carpeted stairs.

Even with the full-length black veil on, people could still see the pink, blistering, Freddy Krueger-looking skin through the fabric. Thanks to Kenna (a make-up artist for indie horror flicks), Brix had a realistic-looking mask that covered her exposed flesh. It was a six-hour tedious process, but one that was well worth the time.

"For those of you who knew Becky, you know how smart,

beautiful, and funny she was," Brix began. "Her character was slandered and put into question before she passed away by the *pigs*," Brix spat, addressing the law enforcement in attendance. "But everyone knows that was a bogus fishing expedition in attempts to frame my family."

"I'm not supposed to be out of the hospital, but I wasn't gonna miss my only sibling's funeral for the life of me. The woman we are burying today was an honest woman. A loyal woman. A giving woman who'd give you the shirt off her back! Becky had heart. A huge heart that rubbed off on whoever was around..." Brix gave a heartfelt eulogy that had everyone in tears. "Luckily, her wish was to be cremated. The way she died handled most of that job for her." People looked around and gasped in shock. "Oh, come on, it was a joke. She would want you guys to smile. When did any of you know her to be sad and down? Never! So, while we mourn her in death, let's celebrate her in life." Brix turned and caressed the gold urn on the podium. She kissed it, and her parents helped her back to the first pew.

After the funeral, Agent Bradshaw and Holis walked up to the Slinkowski's outside of the church. "Deeply sorry for your loss sir," Bradshaw addressed Tom. "On behalf of the FBI, I would like to tell you we are dropping all charges against your daughter."

"Are you fucking kidding me? She's dead, you moron!" Gail shouted at Bradshaw. She snatched the urn from Brix. "You wanna bring charges against a pile of ashes you fuckwad? Leave my fucking family alone. You've done enough damage to our reputation."

"I apologize for any inconvenience your family had to go through but –"

"Look, pal. We want a formal letter of apology, and a representative from the motherfucking FBI, to give an oral apology to the *press*, announcing my daughter's innocence," Tom told him.

"Um, that might be a stretch. But we just wanted to tell you we're closing Becky's case and leaving your family alone. And again, our deepest condolences." Bradshaw said and began to walk away.

"Psssh, now you wanna leave us alone? Get da fuck outta here!" Brix said.

"We're sorry. We'll be on our way," Agent Holis said.

"The nerve of those people," Gail Slinkowski spat. Close friends rubbed her back and calmed her down while Tom signaled for their black limo. Brix was wearing some big, oval-shaped Chanel sunglasses with mini-cameras in them. Beneath her veil, she was able to give the BBC a live feed of all the attendees at the funeral. They knew there would be cops, Feds and other law enforcement agencies there, so they chose to not attend. But they did need to see faces and hear voices for their own research, so they showed Brix how to work the 007-like shades.

Agent Bradshaw thought it would be good to apologize *personally* to the Slinkowski family. After all, it was his narc that set up their daughter. And now that Becky was dead, and their only other child was burned to a crisp, they didn't need any more stress. But his decision to address them put him in the crosshairs of some very strategic and bad ass chicks.

~

"Damn my nigga, you done let your shit get all bama and shit," Telly Da Barber said.

"Yeah man, I been laying low for a min," Travis said and sat in the chair. They were at Ebony Man's World, one of Milwaukee's best Barbershops. "Plus, *this* nigga been wanting me to bring him wit me, once his babyface ass grew a few strands," Travis laughed and pointed at his cousin Lil Mace.

"Aw, nigga fuck you. Don't be mad cuz da hoes like my pretty shit mo then yo ugly ass," Lil Mace responded and laughed.

"Psssh, whatever nigga. Anyway, get cha boy right Telly." Travis reclined in the chair as the black nylon barber's cape was draped over him.

"I gotchu my nigga. I'm gon have you real right when you leave up out dis muhfucka." Telly assured Travis and pumped the chair up higher. "Yo, just sit in that chair fam," Telly told Lil Mace, pointing to the empty chair next to his work station. "My nigga Kal gon plug you reeeeeeal nice."

"Bet!" Lil Mace said, rubbing his palms together excitedly. Ever since the beard craze took over, he'd been wanting to grow a nice crispy one. But because he had a "babyface," it took him a lot of shaving just to get his facial hair to grow in.

As was customary in all barbershops across America, their necks were taped with white paper, and the mood was set to gossip.

"So, what's been poppin out here dog?" Travis asked.

"Man, same 'ol shit. Muhfuckas getting money and dying, and not being able to find no weed around here," Telly Da Barber said, powering up his clippers.

"Word? I ain't know it was dry round dis muhfucka."

"Dry as porn bitch pussy!" Telly said.

"You mean old bitch pussy," Travis corrected him.

"Naw nigga. I know some old hoes whose pussy gets wet as a muthafucka! I'm talking about them *porn* hoes. Them bitches fuck so much they pussy don't even get wet no mo. Do you ever watch porn? Them hoes take all that dick and they walls be dry and beat up as a bitch!"

"Umm ok," Travis said, confused. "So, you ain't got no gas?"

"Hell naw, niggas been selling that homegrown bullshit lately."

"Shiiid, we got some fire ass smoke," Lil Mace interjected.

"Oh yeah, lil buddy? Well, I need a few bricks of it. Not a zip or two," Telly told him.

"Nigga we got that! What you want, ten, twenty, thirty?"

"Shut cho ass up fool," Travis scolded Lil Mace. "Um, I can plug you wit something if you let me know what you need," he told Telly.

"Bet. Let me see what my bitch wanna do." Telly grabbed his phone and sent a text. When he "accidentally" moved the cape so that Travis' arm was exposed, he took a few pics. "She gonna let me know how much bread I'm working wit. But I know fa sho I'll grab at least ten of them."

"Cool. I got chu. Mace. Hit Russ and tell him to put me a ten-piece dinner on standby."

"Aight," the young hustler said, already texting the plug.

"Heyyy, who want some drank?" A tall dreadlocked dude said, entering the shop. He held up a bag full of liquor bottles as he puffed on a blunt.

"Perfect timing my nigga. Y'all sip?" Telly asked his customers.

"Hell yeah!" Travis and Lil Mace shouted in unison.

"Cool. Yo, this is Peru. He gonna hook you up fam," Telly said to Lil Mace.

"Huh? I thought you said yo nigga Kal was gon plug me real nice."

"Oh, he is. He gon' give you the hot towel and the crispy straight razor joint. Peru finna taper you up and get cha head right."

"Oh, alright," Lil Mace said and settled into the barber chair.

Peru pulled a bottle of Hennessey and some red paper cups

from the grocery bag. He filled four cups half-way with the brown drink.

"So, what chy'all been choppin' it up about?" Peru asked.

"Shit, man. I said death and money is the same 'ol same shit going on around here."

"Yeah, but look, that shit can happen to anybody. You see how Pill Mobb went out," Peru said, passing the blunt to Telly.

"Maaaaan, now ***that*** shit was nuts dog. That ain't no everyday shit. Neither is how Kobe went out either...damn, it's been some crazy ass deaths lately," Telly passed the blunt to Travis. "Move your head dis way."

"Yo, who is Pill Mobb?" Travis inquired, as he puffed on the blunt with his head tilted.

"Fam, you close my shop down for some niggas who don't know who Pill Mobb is? Telly, do you know how much money we turned away?" Peru said.

"Huh? Wait... *your* shop?" Lil Mace said.

"Yeah, lil nigga. I *own* this muthafucka. I also cut hair in this bitch. It's mo ways than one to get it right?"

"You're right school, you right. Damn, that's what's up."

"Look, my guy. I ain't know who owned this muhfucka. But I hit your man's with some bread so we can have our privacy in dis bitch. Now, I don't know what that got to do with knowing who da fuck Pill Mobb is, but –"

"You're right. Telly obviously was compensated enough to close shop for y'all. Um, what they call you my guy?" Peru asked.

"Tray-eight Trav. And that's my cousin Lil Mace."

"Aight then. Y'all just kick back and chill Tray-eight Trav. Smoke, drink, get crispy. Y'all want me to call some bitches to come through?" Peru asked. His back was to them, he looked at their heads in the mirror while he doused two of the cups with a clear liquid.

"Hell yeah. Long as they bussin' down, I ain't trying to talk and cuddle. I wanna fuck and gone bout my business bitch," Lil Mace said. All the guys laughed.

"Fa sho. I know some hoes that only wanna suck, get fucked, and bounce!" Peru said.

"Now ***them*** my type of bitches. Call them hoes up dog," Travis interjected.

"Say no more," Peru handed everyone their cups and raised his in the air. "To getting off and getting gone!" They all toasted and drank.

"You really ain't heard of that Pill Mobb shit my nigga? Them the whiteboys who burned up at the show in Appleton," Telly said to Travis.

"Oh yeah, I heard something about that, but wasn't that a rock group? They said it was some fireworks and special effects shit right? I still don't know who Pill Mobb is my nigga."

"Pill Mobb was them niggas, my nigga! They a whiteboy rap group. But they was new tho, so only them suburban kids knew about them. Fam, them niggas went out like *gangstaz.* Set theyselves on fire to their song saying they on fire," Telly said excitedly.

"My nigga, if it ain't Eminem –"

"This nigga made all they beats too," Telly cut Travis off. "This nigga is a platinum-selling producer, my nigga," Telly pointed at Peru who just smiled and raised his cup.

"School. You cut hair, own the shop you cut hair in, *and* do beats?" Lil Mace asked.

Peru gulped his drink and sat the empty cup down. "Yup, grind mode young blood. I gotta get every dollar I can get. If you know some lil rappin muthafuckas, send 'em my way. I'll turn 'em into stars..."

BY THE TIME the women showed up, the barbershop was a smoke-filled party lounge. Music banged from the bass speakers and they were on the second Hennessey bottle. Tray-eight Trav and Lil Mace were beyond inebriated thanks to the Mickey Peru slipped them.

"And what's your name baby?" Cat asked Lil Mace. He looked at the half black, half Russian stunner with the sexy accent. This was a whole new breed of foreign to him.

"I'm Lil Mace. But ain't nothing little about me," he said, feeling himself.

"Oooh, Daddy. I feel you on that." Cat said and straddled him in the barber chair. She put her feet next to his knees and wrapped her arms around his shoulders. Lil Mace palmed her juicy butt and smiled like a kid in a candy store.

Nymphy was giving Travis a lap dance in the other chair. Summer, GG, and Lyza, were lounging on the leather sofa, caressing on Telly and Peru.

"You see my nigga. These hoes buss down thotianas for real!" Peru said, smacking GG on her butt.

"Heyyyyy," GG got so excited from getting her butt slapped, she twerked it with glee.

"Yeah, this what I'm talking about," Lil Mace beamed as Cat crawled under the barber's cape and pulled his dick out. She licked it up and down, and he threw his head back.

"Is that how the hoes do it where you from Papi?" Rose whispered in Lil Mace's ear. "Do they look you in your eyes when they suck you off? Do they gag on it and leave spiderwebs of spit on your dick like..." Cat pulled Lil Mace's dick out of her mouth. She ripped the cape off and threw it on the floor. She held his piece inches from her face while she looked up at him. A bridge of saliva from the tip of his dick to her bottom lip swung in the air. "Where are you from Papi?" Rose asked him before sucking on his earlobe lightly.

"Ph-ph-phoenix," Lil Mace stuttered. Cat dove in, deep-throated his pole, and swallowed him whole like a pill. "Damn bitch, you a muthafuckin beast! Shiiiiid."

"That's what I thought," Rose patted him on the shoulder and walked off. She stood next to Travis and observed the show Nymphy gave him. Her long Sioux hair whisked back and forth, grazing his knees whenever she threw her head back in ecstasy.

"Can you call for another ten?" Rose asked Travis.

"Hu-uhn? Wh-whoa girl!" Travis tensed up. Nymphy's hand found its way to his dick.

"She can go get the money real quick if you can have 'ol boy do another ten," Telly said, walking up to them.

"Shit, my nigga. We gotta do this right now? Can't we handle it later?" Travis sighed. He was in the middle of sucking some nice titties when Rose interrupted him.

"These bitches ain't going nowhere my nigga. This money, however, don't wait for ***no*** one. It's whoever go get it. That's what makes a go-getter," Rose said.

"Is you a go-getter my nigga?" Telly asked him.

"Hell yeah fool. But I don't party like this every day. Damn, y'all got it poppin in dis bitch! A nigga rollin, the hoes got they titties out, mannn..." Trey-eight Trav grabbed his phone and sent a text. "I'll see. He might not have ten tho."

"We'll take whatever you got. This some *gas*. And with it being so dry around here, we wanna make sure we got some on deck." Rose threw her two cents in.

"I'll see what my mans say. Damn, I'm fucked up in this piece," Travis slurred.

"I'm coming! I'm comiiiiiiiing!" Lil Mace announced. Cat stepped back and watched his penis shoot fountains of nut in the air. He was so happy. He didn't even mind that it got all over his clothes.

"Yeah, my dude said he'll bring another ten in like twenty," Travis read the text out loud.

"Cool, invite the nigga in this time," Rose said.

"Yeah, fam. Russ gotta try shorties head game," Lil Mace

said as he pulled up his pants. "Hey OG, can I still get that hot towel treatment?"

"Yup, fam coming through any min...wait, here the nigga is now," Telly replied. A stocky dark-skinned dude walked into the barbershop "Bout time. We been waiting on you for hours!"

"My bad dog. I had to holla at my Hampton niggas about something," Kal said.

"Hamp? Yo, do you know them Bodygang niggas by chance?" Travis asked.

"Fool stop it. Show and killa nem? Them my muhfuckas."

"Word? Man, them rapping ass niggas some animals foolie," Travis commented.

"Who you telling? So, who getting the hot towel demo?" Kal asked.

Lil Mace raised his hand. "Let me get myself together first OG," he said, zipping up his jeans. "Y'all got a washroom a nigga can use?"

"Bathroom is the first door on your left," Kal said, pointing to the back.

"Daddy, I wanna ride your dick like it's a mechanical bull. But first I wanna suck on it. Can a bitch suck it for a little bit?" Nymphy asked.

Travis looked at his watch. "Damn! Yeah baby, just wait til my man's come through to handle dis bidness, then we can do whatever," he said rubbing on her booty.

"Ooooh yes. I'll take these off then," she said and got completely nude. No one batted an eye at the dime-piece native chick undressing in the middle of the barbershop. Travis was hypnotized, and when Lil Mace came out of the bathroom, he stopped in his tracks and stared at her pretty self.

"Dammmmn, can I have some of that too?" Lil Mace asked, rubbing his crotch.

"Mhm, sho' can. One in my pussy, and one in my mouth. Whenever you ready."

"Bro, I *like* these hoes. They bout that life!" Lil Mace said. He just didn't know how "bout that life" those women were. More drinks were poured, more blunts were lit, and everyone was zoned out when Russ came through with the weed.

Rose counted the money out and exchanged it with Russ for the duffle bag. "Have a seat my nigga. We gotta talk," Rose pulled a gun out and put it to the drug dealers head. His fitted cap fell to the floor as he put his hands up.

"Yo, what da –" Lil Mace pulled his pistol out and started to walk up but GG was on him like stink on shit.

"Ah ah ahhh lil dog," GG warned as she disarmed him.

"Telly man, how you –"

"Shut da fuck up nigga," Lyza silenced Travis with the silencer she put in his mouth. ***Pfft.*** She squeezed the trigger and painted Telly Da Barbers whole workstation and mirror with Travis' brains.

"Shit! Yo, look. Y'all can have that weed. You ain't gotta kill a nigga over dis shit," Russ pleaded. Tray-eight Trav's limp body was pushed on the floor, and they made Russ sit in the bloody chair.

GG and Summer led Lil Mace back to the chair he had an orgasm in. "Cute gun you got here lil homie. You know how to use it?" Summer said and put the young man's gun to his nose. If he hadn't been wearing red jeans, the pee stain that grew by the second wouldn't have been noticeable. "Awww, did the Lil guy piss in his True's?" Summer taunted.

"Aight. We already know y'all the niggas that robbed our girl. Now, what we want to know is, who sent y'all to do it?" Rose said aloud as she paced in front of their two captors. "And please don't play no games with me. My girl over there has an itchy ass finger I tell ya."

Russ and Lil Mace looked at each other, then stared at their dead friend on the floor.

"Look ma, we just got wind of a lick and –" ***Pffft Pffft Pffft.*** Lyza shot Russ in the chest, neck, and face, mid-sentence.

"Daddy, I don't think these bitches are playing," Cat told Lil Mace. "Bullshit ain't nothing, if I was you, I'd tell them what they wanna know. Two of your boys already slumped. Shiiid," she smacked her lips and popped some chewing gum.

"Alright, alright. I'll tell y'all whatever y'all wanna know. Just please let a nigga walk up out of here. I'm only twenty-two. I ain't *seen* shit yet," Lil Mace whined.

"Aight Lil homie. You have my word, you'll walk out this muhfucka if you keep it one-hunnid wit us," Peru said, and patted the frightened young man on the shoulder.

"Thank you Jesus," Lil Mace sighed and sat up straight in the chair. "Ok. This nigga Neef was telling our boy Terrance about some bitch named Carol. I guess she was one of his niggas sister or some shit. Anyway, word gets back to this nigga that his sister is in Milwaukee. The bitch took a case for the nigga and he wanted to know where the fuck she was at, and why didn't she tell him she was out the joint."

"Bro, what da fuck is you talking about?" Kal asked, getting frustrated.

"Naw, naw, hear him out," Rose interjected.

"Thanks ma. So, check it. Terrance runs into the bitch on a humbug when he was kickin' it with Neef. She didn't remember him because he was like every other tatted up thug nigga back home, but he knew *her*. As soon as he saw those buttermilk cheekbones, he said 'yup. That's bro's sister.' She ran guns for them when she was a snot nose. Small world right? Bitch was so high; she ain't even realize she was kicking it wit a muhfucka who taught her the game. They had a coked-out orgy or some shit with a thick Asian bitch –"

"Ma Baby," GG said.

"Yeah, *dat* bitch. Anyways, Terrance goes back home for Christmas and tells bro she's in the Mil. Trav is my big cousin on my sister's auntie's mama side. Figured we'd use another body for the lick since he was from here. Then bro did this mulatto James bond pimp move type –"

"Bruh, mulatto James Bond?" Summer questioned.

"Yeah! Pimp player move type shit. He came to the Mil knowing 'ol girl walked her Russell Terrier at the dog park every day."

"Wait, wait, wait, a minute muthafucka. The dog park? That's where Chula met –"

"**GOLDY!**" Everyone in the room shouted.

"So y'all already know it was her baby daddy that sent us up in there then," Lil Mace exhaled and felt better.

It turns out, the Bad Bitchez Click weren't the only ones who could make major chess moves. Once Carol's brother found out his sister was free, he did his own "release plan." He came all the way from Phoenix and set up a low-key spot on the southside of Milwaukee. With him being mulatto, he blended in well with the various Hispanic hues that populated the south.

By the time he met Chula at the dog park, no one had seen or heard from Carol. He figured it was bogus information Terrance gave him until he found out Chula sold weight. Always on a come up, he'd hit up his goons in "da 'Nix" to hit Chula for her shit. While Goldy knew for sure his sister would hit him up if she was out, his grimy plot to rob his babymama solidified why his own blood didn't fuck with him. He was bottom tier cut-throat — pure scumbag.

As promised, they let Lil Mace walk out of the barbershop. GG even gave him his gun back on the way out. He was scared shitless, but happy as hell that they let him up out of there. All his niggas got merked up in there. Damn, he told them though, he was only twenty-two...

As he pulled off in his white on white Lexus, Kal popped up from the backseat.

"I told you I was gon get you reeeeeal niiiiiice!" Kal hissed in Lil Mace's ear then sliced his throat with an ivory-handled straight razor. Blood covered the windshield like it went through a gory car wash. Lil Mace coughed and gagged as he tried to breathe through a severed windpipe. His hands attempted to close the red sea parting from his neck, but they couldn't get past his shoulders. His life pumped out slowly as his head slumped against the steering wheel. Kal reached over and threw the car in park. "Hey, at least you gon look crispy in da casket my nigga," he said and got out the car.

10

Sex, Mystery & Mayhem

Chula didn't know the man she fell for was also her ex-lovers' brother. He played a great role trying to find his sister. Chula thought he was just a sexy ass hustler from the dirty; she found out the hard way, that he actually *was*.

"To my fiiiiiine ass babydaddy y'all!" Chula shouted from the back of the limo. She raised her champagne glass high in the air. The whole gang was in the stretch limousine, on their way to Summer's sex toy release show.

"Girl quit putting a nigga on blast," Goldy said. He was high as hell from the blunts BBC were rolling up. It was one thing for Chula to invite him to her friends' sex toy party. But the fact that she wanted him to pick their next threesome partner was enough to get him out of the house for the night.

"Naw boo, she ain't lying," GG said and caressed his face.

"Nigga, you know you fine as hell, with your pretty ass. You better enjoy the compliments why they last," Lyza told him.

Goldy smiled like he won the lottery. Besides him, there were only two other men in the bad bitch-filled limo. And all the women were on ***his*** nuts.

"Anyways, a bitch trying to show you some love nigga. Soak that shit up," Chula said.

"Aight, aight. That's what's up boo. Good looking, I appreciate it."

"Yeah, nigga. Sit back. Check out my homegirls. See which one you wanna take back to the crib with us –"

"Just one?" Goldy questioned hopefully.

"Boy, don't play with me," Chula warned him.

"Whaaaaa? You got some bad ass friends. Look at all these fine muthafuckin' women in this limo. You ain't never introduced me to half these bitches before." Goldy said and looked around the limousine. They were going to a major event, so everyone was fitted to death.

His baby mama was the most casual because she was pregnant. She wore a maroon Chanel gown and matching Uggs. As bad as she wanted to rock her maroon YSL Crocodile heels, she just couldn't put her feet through that for several hours with a "bun in the oven."

Lyza wore a red, low-cut dress with a plunging neckline and heels. GG and Rose wore the same backless Gucci dress, but they were different colors (Rose in pink, GG in Purple). Quintasia wore thigh-high black leather boots with dozens of zippers on them, and a lace panty and bra set underneath a waist-length Chinchilla. Nadia wore a hundred-dollar bill embroidered dress and mint Timb boots with hundred-dollar bills all over them.

Everyone couldn't wait to see what Summer was going to wear. She told the gang she was going to do something extravagant. She was already at the Fiserv Forum Arena with Angelo, making sure everything was ready for her "Duck Me" Sex toy release party. There were a lot of media outlets there to document her revolutionary sex toy and she wanted everything just right.

This was the first outing Nacho attended with his babymama (even though she brought her main dude Neef with), and Nacho was letting his presence be felt.

"Well, why y'all toasting to this niggas looks, I want to make a toast to a legendary evening. Our girl Summer is doing big thangs. Here's to further success," Nacho said.

"To further success!" Everyone repeated and raised their drinks.

"Hey fam, no disrespect to you," Nacho addressed Goldy, then turned to the women. "But *fuck* you bitches if you think I ain't dripping sauce in this muhfucka," he said and lit a blunt. Nacho wore a tie-dye Versace shirt with Medusa and snakes on it, some grey leather pants, and a Stacy Adams fedora. On his feet were $1,000 Versace Baroque Chain Cross sneakers.

Neef, who was hugged up with Ma Baby, wore a colorful Coogi outfit and turquoise Havana Joe boots. His jewelry was just as colorful, as he rocked four chains (two with huge iced out medallions), a Rolex, a chunky bracelet, and a few rings adorned his fingers.

"Whatever boy. You flexing, ain't nobody denying that" GG told Nacho. "But fuck all that, put that movie on Chu. Shiiiid, we going to a sex toy party at the Bucks Arena, we might as well set the mood."

Chula put a DVD in the portable player, and within seconds all six TV's in the limo showed three sexy women fondling each other.

"Mmmmm, you have a magical tongue," Carol moaned. The camera zoomed in on the cute mulatto girl's face which was scrunched up in ecstasy. The two highest people in the limo (Ma Baby and Goldy), immediately sobered up and sat up straight. Everyone stared at a screen near them as erotic moans came out of the speakers.

"You like that baby?" Chula asked from between Carol's legs.

"Mhmmmmmm," Carol ran her fingers through Chula's long brown hair and gasped.

GG came into the video and sat on Carol's face. "I want to get in on this. Ooh shit, lick that gushy ass pussy like it's your last meal bitch. Yeah, Carol. Thaaaaat's it."

"What the fuck?" Goldy yelled and spilled his drink.

"What's wrong daddy? I Thought you liked to see your girl with other chicks?" GG said.

Goldy looked from the TV to Chula to GG. "H-h-how? Where? Chu, what the..." Goldy was baffled.

Ma Baby was also in her own stunned daze. Her heartbeat sped up, seeing Carol on the video like that. All the women in the Limo searched her face for signs, but she didn't reveal anything besides shock.

Chula smiled. "Yeah. That's my girl, Carol. Well; *was* my girl. She ain't been around in a while. Damn shame too. That little bitch could eat pussy like it's *nobody's* business. She was most def a good sub. You taught her well Ma Baby."

"Y-y-you know my sister? Where is she?" Goldy angrily asked Ma Baby.

"Your sister? What the fuck is you–"

"Yeah," GG said, cutting Ma Baby off. "This nigga right *here* is none other than Jermaine "Goldy" Coleman. Carol's big brother."

"How the fuck you know? Chula, what the hell is going on?"

"You're good my nigga. I really thought you were into me. Here it is, you've been on some undercover shit this whole time trying to find your sister. Well, you're too late."

"Whatchu mean 'too late' Chula? Where's my sister? And who the fuck is she?" he pointed at Ma Baby.

"Look fam, you ain't finna be all hostile towards my girl," Neef said. Ma Baby put a hand on Neef's chest to calm him down while she tried to figure out her next move. Luckily for her, they pulled up to the front of the Bucks Arena before she could process her thoughts.

"I CAN'T BELIEVE you talked me into coming to this thing," Christine Holis said. Her sister Courtney had seen the promos for the "Duck Me" sex toy online. Even though she was an avid heroin user, Courtney could only orgasm with toys, so she was a dedicated collector of them.

"Hey, you always say we never do anything together. Well, it's sister's night out, so enjoy it!" Courtney said, looping her arm through her sister's. They joined the thousands of other people piling into the arena. The turnout was massive, and the outcome would be legendary.

"DADDY, WE GOTTA GET OUTTA HERE!" Ma Baby whispered to Neef as they entered the loud Arena. Nacho walked closely behind them, so she made sure to keep their convo on the low.

"Why? We just got here. We ain't even seen yo girl yet," Neef responded.

"Yeah, fuck all that. It's some funny shit going on boo," Ma Baby said skeptically.

"You talking about that nigga in the Limo? Fuck dude! Who cares if you were fucking his sister? She was obviously bussin' down for them other hoes too. I wouldn't worry about it."

Ma Baby shot daggers at Neef and sighed. Out of her peripheral, she tried to watch all the women they came in with. She didn't know them and didn't trust them as far as she could throw them. Ma Baby texted her Milwaukee Mami's and took a deep breath.

~

"HEYYYYY Y'ALL! THANKS FOR COMING," Summer announced and hugged all of her peeps. While all the other attendees had to sit in the stands, Summer had reserved seats on the floor for her crew. As promised, Summer left nothing to the imagination. She looked like a naughty schoolgirl dominatrix. Her hair was in pigtails, rubber ducky pasties covered the nipples of her exposed breasts, a leather mini-skirt covered half her butt cheeks, and baby blue snake-skin boots were on her feet. She was covered in a shimmering glitter that made her golden skin radiate.

"Giiiiiirl, you look hot as fuck! Looking like a bad ass redbone Harley Quinn," Lyza said.

"Hell yeah mami. Look at you," Rose commented and licked her lips unconsciously.

"Thanks ma. But what about my ***man***? Ain't he fly as a muthafucka? This the *real* Italian Stallion right here," Summer gushed and pulled Angelo into the conversation.

He wore a white Armani suit with emerald cuff links and shiny Italian shoes. "Summer, please darling. This is *your* night hun," Angelo blushed.

"Angelo, you always looking good boo," GG expressed, after she hugged him.

"Thank you GG. You as well."

"Hey Ma Baby. How you been girl?" Summer asked and smiled as best she could. The hate she had for the snake bitch was so strong, she thought Ma Baby could see it in her eyes.

"I been good. I'm super proud of you girl. This shit is biiiig," Ma Baby said. She had never been to the new arena, so she was astounded when she looked around the huge place.

"Thanks. Yeah, it's been a long time coming, but tonight is the muthafuckin night! Bullshit ain't nothing, we bout to kill shit with this," Summer held up one of her vibrating ducks and smiled. "Y'all can get comfortable in them chairs. I'll be starting the presentation shortly. I'm having a raffle too. Giving away lots of prizes. One dollar a ticket. Get 'em before they sell out. And if y'all want some party favors, go behind that V.I.P. Cabana over there," Summer pointed to a curtained-off section that had a red velvet rope around it. "There's TVs and shit in there. Y'all can watch what's going on from inside there if you don't feel like being ogled by thousands of peering eyes. Don't fuck with them trunks though, they're for the magic show."

There was a massive stage set-up center court. Behind the stage was a 100-seat section with various musical instruments on the seats. In front of the stage, Summer had 50 seats reserved for her peeps. Everyone else was to sit in the stands. There were special Cabanas roped off for various purposes for the show.

"Bet girl," Ma Baby said. "I show ain't trying to have all these muthafuckas all up in mines! Can we smoke in there?"

"Shiiid, as much money as I dropped on this event, you can do any and everything but *kill* a muthafucka behind there," Summer laughed.

Ma Baby tensed up at her comment but played it off. The video of Carol was still lingering in her thoughts. She looked at GG and Chula. GG smiled at Ma Baby. *What the fuck is she on? And how long was she fucking my bitch behind my back?* Ma Baby pondered to herself. "Ok Summer, good looking ma. Here, can you get me some of those raffle tickets? Me and my boo finna cozy up in the cabana," Ma Baby peeled off two hundred-dollar bills and handed them to Summer.

"Bitch, she got a show to put on," Nacho said and snatched the money from Ma Baby. "I'll go get 'em. I want some anyway.

What's the grand prize Summ? I ain't trying to win that damn duck toy either."

"But Papi... the Duck Me will give you *such* a great orgasm," Rose teased her cousin.

"Shut the fuck up Rose!"

"Calm down kids," Summer laughed. "Y'all something else. Anyway, underneath that sheet is a 2020 Cadillac XT6. Apple red and fully loaded. Some lucky person is gonna win that bad boy tonight," Summer informed them.

"Worrrrrd? Hell yeah, I'm buying every raffle ticket left," Nacho said and walked off.

"Uh-uh, nigga. I'm coming with. That lac is mine!" Quintasia said. A couple of the other women went with Nacho and Quintasia to the lobby and entered the raffle.

"What's good Goldy? You aight? You look like you seen a ghost fam," Summer turned her attention to Chula's baby daddy. He stood off to the side with his hands in his pockets and chewed on his lower lip.

"Huh? Uh, yeah, I'm...I need a drink," Goldy replied and walked off.

"Me too! Come on daddy," Ma Baby grabbed Neef's arm and headed toward the cabanas.

Summer waved up at the skybox and everyone turned to see why she smiled so big.

"Girl, is that Giannis?" Rose asked Summer.

"Mhm. The one and only. This is his building. And his name *is* Greek the ***freak***. So you know damn well he was gon' put in an appearance for this ***freaky*** ass event; in *his* house."

"Mm, mm, mm! That nigga *know* he fine. And that accent. Shiiiid, he can get it!" GG said.

"Giiiirl, you ain't never lied," Nymphy joined in. Everyone stared at the seven-foot young legend as cameras zoomed in on him and broadcasted his smile on the Jumbo-Tron.

Summer looked around her vicinity and nodded. "All is clear y'all," she said and hit some buttons on her iPad.

With their main ops out of ear shot, the BBC, THOT Gang, and TLB huddled up and went over their final plan one more time. It was time to checkmate some motherfuckers.

THE STAGE that took up half of the Milwaukee Bucks Basketball floor wasn't just any old stage. It was part entertainment, part dancefloor, and part runway...

100 beautiful women in various designs from the BBC clothing line *BEEast Sting*, strutted the runway. They proudly modeled the sexy garments with flirty walks, sassy hips, jiggly butts, flirty smiles, and genuine waves. Once the last model left the stage, Summer appeared holding her custom microphone with the iced-out beehive handle.

"Is Milwaukee in the houuuuuuuse?" She asked. Loud screams filled the arena. "I want to thank y'all for coming out to the Duck Me release party. I know a lot of y'all don't know me, but I am the creator of this..." Summer waved the microphone at the Jumbo-Tron and the lights dimmed.

WHEN YOU WANT someone to take you, ravish you, make you ***FEEL*** *something, what is it that you're really craving?*

A woman in a bubble bath raised a soapy leg in the air and wiggled her painted toes. A rubber duck floated by, lingering between her tan legs while she soaked. The sexy voice-over continued...

YOU WANT TO BE FUCKED! Admit it. You don't want to swoon and make love when there is a lust throbbing in your loins. A beast in a cage that needs immediate release.

A MANICURED HAND came from beneath the water and grabbed the rubber ducky. It squeaked happily as it transformed.

IT DOESN'T MATTER who you are, or where you are...when that beast is ready to unleash? It's gonna erupt! And whoever, or WHATEVER is around, is subject to...

THE RUBBER ducky disappeared between the woman's legs and bubbles began to circulate like jacuzzi jets were turned on. A deep vibrating bass filled the arena. The woman in the bathtub thrashed about as she moaned and groaned passionately. When she orgasmed, her feet grabbed the faucet. The screen went black for a few seconds.

JUST DUCK ME ALREADY. Duck me and Duck me hard. Duck me like you've never ducked another human being before. Duck me down and Duck me good. I want and need to be Ducked!

A PHALLIC SHAPED duck appeared on the screen. Its beak lit up with LED lights and rotated like an electric toothbrush.

A spotlight was cast onto Summer as she walked the stage and spoke into the microphone. "This is the fastest, most powerfully durable sex toy in the world! With over 20 speeds and patterns, the Duck Me delivers the kind of scratch you need to get rid of that itch. It's Voice-operated, Bluetooth compatible, and you can charge it up with a USB. You can get the single or dual head one, for those of you who want something *different*. Ladies, you'll never be the same after Duck me." All the women in the arena cheered and whistled.

"We're about to see who won this Raffle before we get into tonight's festivities though. Y'all ready Milwaukeeeeeee? Who ready to win some cash prizes?" Summer said and the crowd erupted in applause. Six muscular men dressed like Roman Emperors came out of the tunnel. They wore white togas, sandals, and reef crowns. They pushed a 100-gallon oil drum to the center of the floor. Summer walked off stage and made a show of caressing the men's muscular arms as she walked past each of them.

"Ok, we have ten main prizes to giveaway. These gorgeous Kings are gonna pull a ticket out of this barrel, and when I call your number, come claim your prize." Summer cranked the handle and the barrel spun round and round. Thousands of blue raffle tickets shuffled around until she stopped it and opened the door. "Boys..."

One man picked a ticket out and handed it to her. She read a number off and a loud scream came from the stands. A middle-aged woman with round glasses found her way to the floor to claim prize number ten; A box of assorted Duck Me toys (different sizes, colors, and textures). Gift nine and eight were $500 gift cards (one for Walmart, one for Best Buy). Summer hired people to dress up in Rubber Ducky costumes, so dozens of her "mascots" helped pass out the prizes and hype the crowd up.

Nacho didn't win the Cadillac, but he did win a new Macbook Pro laptop. Courtside season tickets were also one of the prizes someone won. A scooter was given away to a young Marquette student who blushed and sweated profusely. A heavy-set gentleman won a laser hair removal gift certificate and sarcastically replied how that was always what he wanted.

"Give it to a woman sir. Maybe that'll help you get laid," Summer retorted.

A trip to Disney world was given out right before the week-long cruise to the Caribbean was won.

"And now ladies and gentlemen, the moment we've *all* been waiting for," Summer said and pulled the black sheet off the Cadillac. Camera flashes and audible gasps filled the Arena. "The winner of this fine beauty right here is..." A handsome Tyson Beckford looking dude drew the final raffle ticket from the barrel. Summer read the numbers off and a piercing scream came from the stands. A skinny white woman stood up and shouted.

"That's me. That's meeee!" She waved her hands in the air and jumped up and down. She grabbed the woman's arm next to her and drug her down the stairs. "Oh my God, oh my God. I can't believe I won," the pretty blond said into the microphone Summer held.

"What's your name hun?"

"Courtney. And this is my sister Christine," she replied.

"I can see that," Summer said. "Y'all obviously twins right?"

"Yes. She's seven minutes older. But I don't give a fuck, cuz I just won me a Caddyyy! Woot, woot!" Courtney Holis pumped her palms to the sky.

MA BABY WAS in the Cabana snorting cocaine off Neef's dick during the raffle. Each Cabana was like a private bedroom (that just so happened to be in the middle of a basketball court). A queen size bed, nightstand, TV, mini-bar and recliner were behind the black-out curtains that gave V.I.P. occupants total anonymity.

Ma Baby looked up to see who won the Caddy and accidentally bit Neef's penis.

"Ouch! Damn girl, what the fuck?!"

Ma Baby jumped up half naked and walked to the TV. She stood there and stared at the two women talking to Summer. She peered out of the curtains and could see the back of the two blonde's heads. Ma Baby gritted her teeth and reached for her phone...

GOLDY AND CHULA were in another Cabana. Goldy had drank an entire bottle of Vodka and was on ten! "Chula. You know my sister? You *fucked* my sister. You...you..."

"What Goldy? I what? I loved you nigga. And you had some fuck niggas rob me?"

"What? Come on ma. You know I would never –"

"Save it. You know what, when I first found out I was a pawn in your little fishing expedition; I was hurt," Chula admitted. "I really was. But I'm a street bitch. I got over it."

"Chu –"

"Uh-uh nigga. You'll get your turn. It's *my* time to talk..."

SUMMER GAVE Courtney the keys to her brand-new truck, and they posed for a pic next to it. She and Christine got in it and checked things out. They pushed buttons, honked the horn, and giggled excitedly...

LYZA, Nadia, Quintasia, GG and Rose entered Chula's cabana. Goldy sat up straight up when the women walked in.

"What's your girls doing in here Chu? We're having a discussion. Do y'all mind?"

"Yeah fuckboy, we do mind." GG spat.

"You know why these women are here Goldy? Huh? Because everyone in this tent, minus two people, was present when your sister died," Chula said and looked him in his eyes.

Goldy stood up quickly. "Wh-what?" A strong presence parted the curtains behind him and grabbed his shoulders. He turned to see who it was but got head-butted instantly.

"Don't you make another motherfucking move," Big Mama Draws warned him.

"Yeah. She was a rat. She got out of prison with the chinky eyed bitch out there," Rose chided. "They agreed to work with the Feds. They have been doing so ever since they touched down. That's why she never contacted you. Lucky you, though."

"Yeah, you wouldn't wanna show up on the alphabet boys' radar, now would you Goldy bear?" Chula admonished.

"Y'all bitches crazy. Let me up out this muthafucka," Goldy fidgeted.

"Nigga, didn't I tell your bitch ass not to move?" Big Mama Draws wrapped her strong arms around Goldy's neck and put him in the sleeper. He went limp in her arms within seconds! When he woke, he found himself tied naked to the bed with a sock shoved in his mouth.

"Gooooooldyyy. Oh, Gooooldyyyy," Chula sang as she kissed his cheeks. "Glad you could join us again. We had to tie you up cuz you were getting just a little too antsy ya know? Anyway. You're right Papi. We *are* some crazy bitches. We do shit liiiike," Chula aimed the remote at the TV and pictures of Carol's torture appeared in a slideshow of gruesome visuals.

Goldy cried real tears seeing what they'd done to his sister. He had no choice but to watch because they stapled his eyelids open with a staple gun. The torture and pain Carol went through was felt by him. He was scared. He knew he was going to die. Looking for Carol had led him to some real ass gangsta bitches that he didn't know existed. His gumshoe plot would cost him dearly.

"I promised you a threesome Papi, and I'm a woman of my word." Chula crawled onto the bed and hiked her gown up around her waist. She sat on Goldy's limp penis and rocked back and forth. It didn't take long for him to rise to the occasion. "Mmmm, now that's my baby daddy y'all. This nigga can get an erection even with death knocking at his door. Yup, a true dog. You no good motherfucker you!" Chula punched him in the face seven or eight times.

Lyza walked up to the bed with a set of dental pliers. She pulled the sock out and propped his mouth open with the metal tool. Lyza got nose to nose with Goldy. "*I'm* the one who did it. *I* killed Carol. With my bare hands." She wiggled her fingers in his face and laughed.

Chula reached between her legs and stroked Goldy's dick until it was fully erect. Once he was hard, she slid him into her molten wetness and rode him while she spoke.

"The things...we did...to your sister? Goooooo," Chula gyrated her pelvis against his and pulled her swollen breasts out. She pinched the nipples and milk squirted on Goldy's face and down his throat. He choked on the sweet liquid and kicked his feet out. They didn't move much because they were chained to wooden posts at the foot of the bed.

"Me, you, plus the baby makes three. There's...ooh, your threesome." Chula shuddered as her pre-orgasm began to bubble up inside. "We filled all three of your sister's holes with things that represented who she was. Oh, fuck yeah," Chula moaned. "So it's only right that we do her brother the same way."

The "trunks" Summer spoke of earlier were big black Magician trunks that she put in each Cabana. They were two-way objects that could hold a human body and look empty at the same time. They had metal latches outside, and secret compartments inside. Rose opened the trunk and pulled out a long, slithering, black, rat snake. She held it in front of Goldy's terrified face while it hissed and snapped at him. He tried to yell but because of the pliers holding his grille open, it sounded like a wounded wolf instead. He looked at the beautiful faces huddled around his death bed. *Who are these bitches?* He cried to himself.

Nadia pulled a gerbil from the trunk and held it by its tail. It squeaked and kicked its little feet while Chula took it from her.

"What do I tell our child?" Chula rubbed her belly with her free hand. "Well, you aren't a rat like your sister. So at least *that's* a good thing...but you're still a fuckboy." Chula released the gerbil and it fell in Goldy's mouth. It scurried down his throat like it was a hole in the ground.

Rose draped the rat snake on Chula's neck. Goldy's penis was still inside of her. He thrashed around (like a fish out of water), because of the live rodent running around inside of him. He shook his head fearfully as Chula let the snake slither down his esophagus slowly. The women watched as the huge reptile could be seen crawling beneath Goldy's skin. His throat. His chest. And when it got to his stomach; it looked like a kid's toy racetrack was zipping around inside of his belly. The rat snake circled around, doing laps and chasing the gerbil until a massive bulge formed below his belly button. It was the snake swallowing the gerbil whole.

"I'm bout to cum Papi, I'm bout to cum. Don't chu dare die til I cum," Chula announced and ripped the pliers from his mouth. She tossed it on the ground along with a few teeth that flew out. Chula hunched over Goldy and rode him with the fierce viciousness of a woman possessed. She felt the ultimate betrayal. And she knew every time she saw their baby, she would think of its father...that ***she*** killed.

Mom, why don't I have a Dad?

Cuz I killed the no good son of a bitch!

That's how that convo would go. She had other plans for that baby's future.

"Yes, yes, oh fuck yasssssssss," Chula climaxed, and Goldy went into cardiac arrest. The women around the bed held him down until his body stopped thrashing. "Damn, I'm show gonna miss that dick," Chula said as she got up.

The girls loaded Goldy's body into the trunk and consoled Chula. "You sure you're going to be alright girl?"

"Yeah. He wasn't the one for me anyway. But everything happens for a reason. I'm gonna have this baby. But I was hoping you'd adopt it Rose. I know it's a touchy subject, but you'd make a great mom. I'm not ready for this shit yet. So, will you?"

Rose was completely taken off guard. She was tongue-tied for a minute. "Are you serious? Mami, what are you gonna do?"

"Shit, if you say ***yes***, I'm gonna push this fucker out in a few months. *Then* I'm gonna try and get my body back in dime-piece shape. *Then*, I'm gon keep getting this money, and whenever you bring the baby around, I'll be Auntie Chula," she laughed.

"Damn mami. I don't know what to say," Rose pondered. She had been thinking about motherhood lately. With all of the BBC's endeavors prospering, she felt like she had the world in her palms. The only thing she was missing was a little bundle of joy. But she was barren; so wasn't no bundle of *anything* coming out of Rose's womb. Knowing the baby would come from one of her greatest friends encouraged her to say yes. "Ok, I'll accept that offer. Damn, I can't believe I'm going to be a *Madre*." Happy tears slid down her cheeks.

Chapter Eleven
The End Is Near

Ma Baby's click arrived at the Arena fully loaded. They were beautiful women, and because of this, they were able to flirt with security and not get searched thoroughly. Ma Baby sent her main lieutenant Apee the text about Christine and her sister. She also told her to bring back up, because she sensed bullshit in the air. Fourteen women of all races entered the spot in high heels, short dresses, and expensive handbags.

They walked into the Arena and were hit on by all the men who came specifically to get at women. Brushing off their advances, the Milwaukee Mami's entered the show and looked around amazed. One had to marvel at such a beautiful space. But they came in on business and got straight to it.

All of the grand prize winners got to chill in their own V.I.P. cabana. Courtney graciously accepted free drinks from cocktail waitresses dressed in Rubber ducky costumes. She and Christine sipped fruity drinks as they giggled and mingled with the other winners.

"Dang, I wish I coulda won that Caddy," a short brunette said aloud.

"Sorry honey but that motherfucker is miiiine!" Courtney responded and twirled the keys in the air.

"Oh, so you're the lucky bitch that won that beautiful vehicle out there?"

"Yup. That would be me," Courtney laughed and high-fived Christine.

"Damn. I never get that lucky. Can I at least sit in it?"

Courtney looked at the twenty-something year old woman. She had a girl next door face, deep dish dimple in her left cheek, shoulder-length curly brown hair, and wire-rimmed green glasses. She looked like every college kid in America. Courtney looked to Christine for her opinion, she shrugged like *why not?*

"Sure. Come on!" Courtney said. All three of them left V.I.P and got into the SUV.

"Wow. This is niiiiiice," the young woman said from the back seat. She looked around in awe. "Tinted windows are nice and dark. Butter soft leather seats... yeah this is dope."

"Thanks. It has a nice sound system too," Courtney informed her.

"Really? Let me hear it," the curious woman said and pulled her phone out.

Courtney turned V100 up and the surround sound speakers came to life. "Hey, what's your name? Maybe we can hangout some time. I'm from Kenosha, but I uh, come up here often."

"Oh, my bad. I'm Alexis."

Courtney turned around in her seat and extended her hand. "Nice to meet you Alexis. I'm–"

"Dead!" Alexis pulled a gun from her purse and fired off two rounds. ***Bang Bang.*** Bullets splattered Courtney's brains against the windshield. Blood dripped on the new seats. Christine was slow to react. By the time she reached for her state-issued, it was too late. ***Bang Bang Bang,*** three shots ripped through the federally's face and left her slumped against the dashboard. The Milwaukee Mami grabbed the key fob and got out of the truck. She chirped the lock button on and grabbed her cellphone.

2 down was the text she sent before she faded into the crowd.

~

THE LIGHTS in the Arena went out and everyone cheered. A harmonic symphony began playing the strings from *Runaway*. When the vibrant strobe lights danced across the stage, it showed a bee shaped swimming pool rising out of it. Steam wafted from the pool and several pairs of legs appeared out of the water.

100 symphony orchestra musicians played music that synchronized swimmers moved to. Water splashed. Feet thrashed. All of it was in sync. A choreographed ensemble that rhythmically went with the hypnotic strings that played.

Women dove out of the steaming pool like dolphins; only to dive back in...like dolphins. They were bikini clad beauties wearing diamond encrusted shark fins on their heads. The crowd ooh-ed, ahh-ed, and took pics and video of the dance/water performance that lasted twenty minutes.

Once the synchronized swimmer demo was over, the pool disappeared back under the stage and thick blue smoke drifted in the air. A 100-foot mechanical Cobra rose from the retracted stage. It was covered in blinking lights and swayed back and forth to the soothing violins and harps that echoed in the arena.

100 Drones (shaped like Beez) came buzzing from every direction. They flew high and low. They circled the Cobra and every square inch of the arena. The Jumbo-Tron played the live footage that the drones captured. People waved, stuck their tongues out, flashed their boobs, and made other gestures to get put on the Jumbo-Tron.

Three white horses walked on stage carrying Summer, Rose, and GG. The women circled the snake prop on their respective horses. "Tonight's theme is one hundred. For those of you who know what keeping it 100 means, I don't have to explain it," Summer said into her sparkling microphone. She and her click had changed into custom snake-skin outfits.

"Plenty of people *talk* that 100 shit. But not many people *live* it," GG continued.

"A lot of people are also afraid of snakes," Rose said. "They are slimy, sneaky, scaly animals. Carnivorous reptiles from the serpent species. And we all know who the *original* serpent was..." Rose dismounted the horse and the Cobras mouth opened up.

Blue smoke came from the long tongue that lowered to the stage. On the tongue, multiple TV screens flashed a series of images.

. . .

MARISOL "MA BABY" Rivera was given thirty years today in Federal court...

PICTURES OF MA Baby from years ago was broadcasted on those screens. Bee drones flew in close to the snake tongue and played the stunning information on the Jumbo-Tron. Nude ballet dancers with snake designs painted on their fit bodies came on stage. They did a dance number, circling the mechanical snake while the clips of Ma Baby's rise and fall was illustrated.

Her trial, incarceration, and welcome home party at the Rave, all played while news reporters spoke about Milwaukee's Latin Queen Pen.

MILLIONS OF DOLLARS in cash and assets were seized...

MA BABY CLOSED the curtain frantically and stared at the TV in her Cabana. She nervously turned to Neef. "Put your clothes on, we gotta get out of here now!"

"Yeah, Ma. You better be riding out. Cuz it ain't looking good for you," Nacho said. He appeared out of nowhere and entered the Cabana.

"Huh? Wh-what?" she stuttered and backed up toward the bed.

Nacho looked the mother of his only child in the eyes. "You're not safe. They know you're working for them people Ma..."

YEAH, she's as dirty as we are. That's why she's our informant, Tyrone Simmons (of Pig Shit) said and laughed. He and

Sedrick were getting lap dances at some Stripclub on the screen. GG recorded their conversation through a camera lens in her necklace. It gave an up-close view of the men's faces while she did what she was best at.

THEY ARE a group of rogue crooked officials that call themselves the Power Squad, aka Pig Shit. Because they are a bunch of dirty cops! They rob, steal, and kill without mercy. And THESE are the heroes you look to serve and protect?

Several members of Pig Shit flashed on the screen. Tyrone, Sedrick, Bradshaw, Christine, and more...

"COME ON. The show finna start. I'm gonna get you outta here," Nacho said.

"Nah, nigga. How do I know I can trust you?" Ma Baby questioned.

"Trust *me?* You got a lot of nerves. You're the damn snitch! But look, you my baby mama. I can't let nothing happen to you. Anita needs her mom," Nacho reached for Ma Baby's arm.

"Uh-uh," she pulled away. "How the fuck are you gonna get me out here Nacho?" Ma Baby demanded.

"I could wheel you out in that trunk," he pointed to the huge box next to the bed. "Then you can sneak out through the exit when we get in the back hall."

"Nigga is you crazy? You ain't putting my bitch in a trunk!" Neef exclaimed.

"Yeah, I ain't going out in that," Ma Baby looked at the big refrigerator sized trunk.

"Alright, alright. Everybody calm the fuck down," Nacho sighed. "I think I have an idea. I'll be back in a sec. Sit tight."

He left and came back seconds later with one of the Rubber Ducky Mascots. He made the man take his costume off and Ma

Baby put it on. Nacho knocked the man out and stuffed him inside the trunk. Nacho told them he'd be right back and left again.

Ma Baby put the yellow head on and adjusted it. "We're gonna get out of here Daddy. We're taking a trip *tonight,*" she told Neef through the furry head.

"That's cool baby. We can hit Mexico, Europe or whatever," Neef responded.

Within minutes, Nacho showed up with another mascot. "Go with her, she'll lead you out the back. Long as you got that costume on you good. Whatever you do, don't take it off." Nacho told Ma Baby.

"What about Neef?" she looked at her boyfriend anxiously. The cocaine in her system made her heartbeat furiously. She could feel the blood pumping through her veins.

"He ain't the one getting put on blast Ma Baby. He'll be meeting you soon. But you gotta go and go now!" Nacho stated. The other mascot grabbed Ma Baby's arm.

"Come on, I know how to get out of here," the soothing voice said and handed Ma Baby a tray of drinks. They exited the Cabana with trays of drinks and waved at the crowd. They looked like a couple of Duck Me mascots going to get more drinks for the V.I.P.'s.

The mascot lead Ma Baby through the tunnel. They jog-walked the length of a football field. The costume weighed 70 pounds, so it was an exhausting feat going down the long corridor.

"In here," the mystery woman said and opened a door marked MAINTENANCE.

They walked inside the Mechanical room full of pipes, electrical equipment and ventilation systems. It was loud, steamy, and musty inside the room.

"There's a boiler room towards the back. It has an exit that leads to the parking structure. You can call your peeps and tell them to pick you up there," the woman said to a winded Ma Baby.

"Hey, thanks a lot," Ma Baby took the six-pound head off and gasped for breath.

"No reason to thank me," she pulled her own duck head off and shook her long blonde hair out. "You should've listened to Nacho. He said don't take that off." The woman turned around and faced Ma Baby; the biggest Snake she'd ever known.

Ma Baby's eyes bulged out of her head. "Buh-buh-Becky? It can't be! I...I thought you were dead," she said in shock.

The woman walked up to her slowly. Ma Baby hadn't seen those blue eyes since that fateful day in Becky's car when she set her up.

"She is. But she told me to give you a message..." Brix sneered and raised a knife...

As soon as Ma Baby left the Cabana, Nacho snapped Neef's neck like a twig.

"Bitch ass nigga. Fuck you and that rat ass bitch," he said, and spit on Neef's dead body before stuffing it in the trunk with the other guy.

"If y'all don't know where the ***fuck***, you at right now. I saiiiiid. Milwaukee..." the arena erupted with energetic chants of Miltown! "Yeah, yeah. Y'all better make some motherfucking noise in dis bitch. I ***said,*** Milwaukee make some motherfucking noise in this bitch," Poobie held the mic next to the .44 on his hip. The whole arena roared with a hometown pride that could only be felt in the heart of the city. Every Milwaukee celebrity that was anybody, was in the building. Sports stars, rappers, the moguls who once *were* rappers, award winning realtors, creative entrepreneurs like Mente, producers of music and indie flicks had their cameras and drones out too, the dope boys were the obvious drippers in their Miltown swag. Jewelry and furs were in abundance (on men and women alike).

"But this ain't bout da Mil right now. Even tho Giannis in da muthafuckin building," Poobie told the crowd. Chants of "Freeek!" resonated in the building.

"Yeah, cuz these next niggas is from two different coasts, and they holding it down!" HD Bolo said into his microphone. The two men were on stage to introduce the next entertainment. The orchestra began playing flutes and harp strings.

Rose gold Rollie on a nigga put the whole whole damn hood on,

Patron of the new I had to put the drip on, ask me how many niggas I done put on...

Roddy Rich appeared in a bucks Jersey and plenty of blinding diamonds. The crowd erupted in applause and excitement. He and A Boogie Wit Da Hoodie performed "*Tip Toe*" (Summer's favorite song). While the young rappers performed for an ecstatic crowd, Ma Baby was bleeding to death on the boiler room floor.

Brix stood over the woman who changed her life. If Becky was never set up, she'd still be alive. And Brix would still be Britney. Ma Baby looked up at who she *thought* was Becky. Those bright blue eyes would forever haunt her in the afterlife. Ma Baby's jugular was sliced in half, making her gurgle and throw up blood as life slowly left her body.

"Becky told me to tell you... she'll see you in hell," Brix pulled a bottle of honey out and drizzled it all over Ma Baby's body. The heart locket around Brix's neck contained some of

Becky's ashes. She opened it and dumped them on Ma Baby's face. It was one of Becky's last requests in her will/video she left behind. She wanted to have her remains placed on the snake bitch that had a hand in taking her out the game. Brix had a sandwich bag full of dead bumble bees and honeybees. She pulled it out and sprinkled them on Ma Baby's twitching body. Brix pulled her phone out and shot video of Ma Baby slowly dying. She pushed send and what happened in the Mechanical room was broadcasted on the Jumbo-Tron.

"Die you snake bitch. Diiiiiie," Brix knelt down and closed Ma Baby's eyes once she took her last breath.

TYRONE AND SEDRICK were told by Gushy that the masterminds behind the Stripclub Capers were the Milwaukee Mami's. Alerted that they would be attending the sex toy party, the two men showed up to observe. They didn't expect to be outed in front of thousands of people. Once the Pig Shit bit came on, they tried to exit as quickly as possible. They almost made it out of the building until some Italian men saying they were security stopped them.

"You two are going to have to come with us," Angelo said in his best American accent.

"What? Hey, we're –" a poisoned dart struck Tyrone in his neck. Sedrick tried to run but got struck with two darts as well.

"Someone get medical out here. We have two people that fainted," Angelo announced.

Women in scrubs and lab coats came with stretchers and hauled the two men off. They would be tortured and butchered by mobsters later.

THE FOURTEEN WOMEN who represented those double M's were

scattered throughout the Arena. The plan was to wait for Ma Baby's word before they opened fire on the Bad Bitchez Click. But as soon as they saw the live murder of their leader, they went into war mode. Gun fire sparked from all sides. They aimed at the stage and fanned shit down. Automatic weapons rat-a-tatted as the mechanical cobra was torn to shreds. Men and women screamed, hid, and fled.

The BBC hit the floor. Bullets ricocheted off the stage as their horses galloped away.

"Fuck you hoooooes!" the woman who killed Christine and Courtney yelled. She ran toward the stage with a Tech nine and let it rip. ***Rrrrrrraaar, Rrrrrraaar.*** Bullets zipped every which away as she stood center court and blasted on her enemies. She was so focused on what was in front of her, she didn't know anyone was behind her. Lyza put a Desert Eagle to the back of the young woman's skull and pulled the trigger. Her body dropped like a leaf.

SUMMER, GG, and Rose grabbed guns from under the stage and shot at every opp who was busting at them. GG stood up and took a slug in the stomach. "Oompf," she dropped her gun and fell on her back.

"GG, you ok?" Rose panicked as she crawled to her wounded friend. Bullets whizzed by their heads at an alarming rate.

"Y-yeah girl. The dress caught it," GG responded. Luckily, they had changed into the bulletproof dresses Angelo provided for them. GG had the wind knocked out of her, but she was still alive.

"Good, let's get out of here. It's about to get ugly," Rose said, and helped GG up. She signaled for the Tryfe Lyfe Bitches nearby to lay down some cover fire. AK-47's and Diamondback DB15's swiss cheesed everything that was shooting at the BBC.

The fatalities were numerous. A few members of THOT Gang and TLB died trying to protect their main ally. Like in every war, innocent bystanders also got hit and lost their lives. The Milwaukee Mami's came in on a *kill and be killed* suicide mission orchestrated by the deceased Ma Baby. She was their cult-like superior that had those women brainwashed like she was Jim Jones or something.

Tires screeched as a Lamborghini truck came barreling onto the floor. It accelerated and braked as it dodged people running for cover. The Driver rolled down the window and emptied a 50-Round Drum on the Milwaukee Mami's still firing shots.

"Giiiiirl, I ain't never been so happy to see you in my *life*," GG gushed.

"I know right? Get in y'all. It's time to blow this popsicle stand," Brix said with a smile. Summer, Rose, and GG got into the whip and reloaded their guns. Brix burned rubber while her click let their enemies have it.

Every single Milwaukee Mami died trying to kill their main targets. They found out the hard way... it wasn't easy to kill a Bad Boss Chick.

THE END

ABOUT THE AUTHOR

Perk Thirty is a multi-faceted writer from Milwaukee, Wisconsin. His passion for books, poetry, screenplays, and music, fuels his creativity in all of those art forms. While "Bad Boss Chicks" is his first official release, there are many more Perk Thirty novels to come.

Through his words, Perk Thirty aspires to take readers on a vivid journey, bringing them out of their current world and into an exciting, entertaining one, if only for a brief time.

For those wishing to discuss Perk Thirty's characters or have special requests, you may write:

Perk Thirty
P.O. Box 1954
Eau Claire, WI 54703

Or you can contact him via Facebook: Perkthirty